Colette

Robert Hart

eBook: ISBN: 978-0-6450169-5-6
Print book: ISBN 978-0-6450169-6-3

Ravensbrück Concentration Camp, 10 am, Thursday 16th November 1944

The cell door crashed open, revealing Vogel in his immaculate SS uniform and I read my end in his arrogant smile.

A guard reached in, grabbing my arm, pulling me to my feet, pushing me down the corridor towards the door to the execution yard. I had watched others take this journey and knew it awaited me. Through the door the sky was a dome of frosty blue, winter sunshine splashing extravagantly onto the concrete walls, honeying their greys. A distant honking pulled my eyes to a pair of elegant geese, sailing above the north German plain towards the Baltic.

The guard stopped and I turned in his grasp. Vogel stood, adjusting the set of his black uniform jacket which he deemed fractionally incorrect. His eyes flicked to the guard, motioning him away. Then his cold eyes found mine.

I stood in a strange calmness, yet a butterfly softly beat its wings in regret, somewhere below my heart.

"There will be retribution."

I spoke a simple truth. Even here in Ravensbrück, news of the Nazi's continuing defeats in both the east and west trickled in but it did not raise hope: hope required energy and we had none. Surviving each hungry, painful, limping day absorbed all our effort. But we knew an end approached, somewhere in the future.

Vogel's lips narrowed to a thin smile, one sardonic eyebrow raised. "You think such a threat will save you?" He spoke excellent English.

I waited before replying, savouring another breath. "I am not trying to save myself." I kept my voice even. "I'm trying to save you."

I saw a flicker in his eye.

A whisper of self-doubt, perhaps?

He stepped back and lifted his pistol from its holster, half-raising it towards me. "Enough. On your knees."

How strange at this moment to recall the anger of Madame Joubert, my Maths teacher, when I giggled as she told me off.

"And if I don't, what then?" I chuckled softly. "You'll shoot me?" The same grim comedy filled this situation, even though the end of it ... was my end.

His eyes narrowed as I held his gaze, taunting him. "Is it difficult to shoot a woman who is staring into your eyes?"

His lips thinned, the pressure outlining them in white. As he stepped forward, the black circle of the pistol barrel grew towards me.

December 1939 – November 1940

When the war broke out, my English father insisted we move back to England. I heard the arguments through my bedroom wall. My mother wanted to stay; she could not countenance leaving her position teaching chemistry at the Sorbonne, her French family and her friends; but my father had re-joined the RAF and England represented safety for the people he most loved.

In the last war, Paris remained free – moving to England for this war seemed unnecessary. I wanted to stay in Paris with all my friends, where I'd spent most of my life. My mother's older sister, and her five children, my cousins, lived in Normandy where I'd spent summer holidays. We'd also visited England of course, staying with my English grandparents on the outskirts of the New Forest west of Southampton, but France – Paris – was my home.

My wishes and those of my mother counted for nought: we left Paris in mid-December 1939, just after my eighteenth birthday. Mother and I went straight to my grandparent's house in Lyndhurst leaving father in London.

My grandparents made us welcome and father joined us for two days at Christmas, rather dashing in his uniform with the droopy RAF wings on his chest, a Squadron Leader's rings on his sleeves. He assured everyone – but principally my mother – that he expected to be posted to a squadron as Intelligence officer or something like that and would not fly operations.

Granny Roberts volunteered with the local Red Cross, helping sort out and care for the children evacuated from London. She scooped us up to help with this and I passed the rest of the winter caring for a group of children from poor East End families. France has poor families, but not on the boulevards of Paris and my grandparents' middle-class world had cocooned me during my visits to England.

These dislocated, scared youngsters from London's east end taught me some of life's realities. Torn away from London, their homes and the people they knew, their world had been shattered. As spring started to bud in gardens and the nearby New Forest, most of the children settled into the countryside life, but a few remained distraught at the cataclysmic change evacuation had brought. Some of the older children asked about returning to London as the war seemed a non-event, with none of the much-feared bombing of cities.

A group of disturbed and restless children of varying ages coalesced around me – perhaps because of my youth, diminutive stature and exotic French accent, signalling that, like them, I belonged elsewhere. They brought me their troubles; I listened and we hugged, sharing fears and tears. A quiet April blossomed into an unwarlike May and the push to return to London became louder.

One morning, I took my group of misfits on a walk into the fields and hedgerows, playing a game with them – they named what we saw and I taught them the French word which they had to remember and say when they saw it again – blackbird: *merle*, sheep: *mouton*. As children of the city, many lacked the English names for what we saw and I had to provide those as well – hawthorne: *aubépine*. We picnicked, eating our sandwiches in the dappled shade of a large oak growing in a hedgerow. When we returned to the Red Cross centre, drawn faces and rising tension greeted us.

Panzers were rolling across France and the low countries.

Through the next weeks, we watched in disbelief as France disintegrated and surrendered. My mother came close to collapse as the *Wehrmacht* swept through our country. Even the miracle of Dunkirk failed to raise our spirits as the unthinkable became a reality: England was next.

This terrifying, existential threat brought great unity of purpose to the country and clarified my thoughts; young and fit, I could contribute so much more than rambling through the fields with a group of evacuees.

I owed France for my happy years of childhood; I was honour bound to repay that debt.

I asked my father about joining the WAAFs – the Women's Auxiliary Air Force. Two weeks later, having stretched to meet the minimum height requirement, I boarded a train to the WAAF training base at Harrogate.

Father had told me that since February, everyone entered the WAAFs at the bottom. This threw together people from all walks of life in basic training – and my education about the real world that started thanks to the East End children continued. I slept in a barrack room with eleven other women – all older than me. I'd never shared a room before and viewed the others in my barrack room nervously. My embarrassment peaked when ordered to strip to my panties while male doctors prodded and stared at me. But my shyness evaporated over the weeks of basic and by the end, I wandered around in undies in the barrack room like everyone else, thinking nothing of it.

In the last week of basic, they listed the jobs open to us, but made it clear that what we wanted counted for nothing against what the country needed. With no real idea about any of the jobs, I thought being a Met Observer, watching and recording the weather, sounded interesting, so I selected that. True to form for the armed forces, which usually confounded the desires of its members, I found myself training as an RDF operator, watching the skies for incoming enemy aircraft. The first thing we learned was that RDF stood for Range and Direction Finding – later called radar – and that it was top secret.

We were reminded about the Official Secrets Act we had signed on joining up.

I took to this specialist training: it piqued my interest and suited my unconventional science background, courtesy of my mother; perhaps the RAF understood me better than I knew myself. Our group of girls worked hard but wanted some fun as well. Our world might end tomorrow and that loosened restraints. The officers watched us closely and suspected every man of harbouring nefarious intent. But as those officers, too, wanted some diversion, we found ways to skirt round them, sneaking off to the local pub and once into town for a dance.

Churchill named the existential conflict in the sky the Battle of Britain. A daily, furious battle raged in the southern skies throughout our training. News filtered through that the Luftwaffe had bombed RDF stations and killed WAAFs, which gave us pause for thought. When a couple of trainees 'washed out' having failed the same test twice, I put my head down and fully applied myself.

We all wanted to work in the thick of it, in one of the RDF stations along the south coast where the big raids were coming in, but at the end of the course the RAF posted me to a place none of us had heard of – Nether Button on the Orkney Islands, north of Scotland. Inevitably, one of my compatriot trainees rudely dubbed it Nether Bottom. I wondered if that's what the people stationed there called it.

Just getting to Nether Bottom ... er Button ... proved quite an adventure involving two days and nights, multiple trains and a ferry. I arrived there at the beginning of September, with the Battle of Britain still raging down south.

Nether Button proved to be the RDF station and a pair of nearby crofters' cottages located about five miles south of Kirkwall, my port of arrival. We stayed in billets in Kirkwall. The RDF station fell under the command of RAF Kirkwall, currently host to a squadron of Hurricanes, but we never saw the station commander. Squadrons rotated through the airfield from the south, each getting a brief respite from the intense fighting while training replacement pilots with great urgency.

The RDF station never closed, its sleepless eye sweeping out across the North Sea towards Norway, enemy territory since April. We worked two four-hour shifts a day in a rotating three-day pattern that nominally provided us with a day off every ten days. But with sickness, transfers and people on occasional leave, shifts varied. Each day we checked the roster before leaving the station for the cold and draughty ride to Kirkwall in the back of a truck and set our alarm clocks for the following shift once we got to our digs.

At the start of the battle, the Luftwaffe sent unescorted bombers on daylight raids from Norway – but guided by our RDF, the fighters mauled them severely. They now only tried that at night. We found this frustrating: we watched them approach on the screens that showed us their position and height. From that we reported the track, altitude and the probable number of aircraft, but the RAF had no night fighters early in the war so the *Boche* carried on unopposed into England and Scotland until their returns faded from our screens. We'd track them again as they flew home having bombed their targets, the ghostly returns mocking our inability to engage.

News from the south suggested our boys were beating the Luftwaffe when they tried big daylight raids against London. But Nether Button stayed quiet and boring, untouched by that drama. This continued as late summer drifted into autumn and then winter, despite the Blitz visiting its night-time horrors on British cities.

Although I spoke excellent English, people noticed my French accent. One grey and windy November morning as I arrived, Sergeant June Ackers (inevitably called 'Ack-Ack', but never to her face) waved at me. "What have you done now, Colette? Flight Officer Marten wants to see you, pronto."

I made my best 'don't know' face, hung up my greatcoat and checked myself in the mirror by the door (Marten was a stickler for this – 'My WAAFs must be properly dressed at all times'). Walking through the hut to our CO's office,

I tried to work out what I'd done wrong but failed to remember anything. Nervous butterflies started up in my stomach. I knocked on the open door and waited.

Flight Officer Marten lifted her head from the papers on her desk. "Come in Roberts. Please shut the door and sit down."

As I sat, the butterflies multiplied their numbers to wing strength, all running up their engines in my stomach.

Why behind closed doors? Had something happened to my father?

F/O Marten picked up a file and flipped through several pages.

"You were born in France, Roberts?"

I blinked, confused, as I expected a reprimand or bad news. "Er ... No, Ma'am. Here in England – in London."

Are they going to kick me out because I'm not English? Heaps of foreigners serve in the RAF – including lots of pilots...

"I'm sorry Roberts – but you are French, aren't you?"

I thought for a moment, disoriented by the direction of her questions. "I'm not sure, Ma'am – I might be both French and English. My passport's British though."

The CO's face crinkled in confusion, so I rushed on. "My father's English but my mother's French. We lived in Paris from before my second birthday – I think – until last December. My parents met when my father flew scouts ... er ... fighters in the Royal Flying Corps in the Great War."

"Hmm." She consulted the file again and then put it on her desk. "You speak French, then?"

How did she think I managed in Paris for 16 years?

I stifled the sarcastic response. "Yes, Ma'am."

She picked up the file on her desk and scanned a page, a frown forming on her forehead. "Well, it seems we need people who speak French." Her eyes narrowed, assessing me. "Are you interested?"

I blinked, trying to get a grip on this. "They don't say why they want French speakers?"

F/O Marten's eyes flicked down to the paper in the file. "No, they don't. But if this interests you, they want to interview you." She smiled. "In London."

Yes. I might get a free trip to London out of this. Get to spend time with my father, perhaps wangle a trip to visit mother in Lyndhurst.

My commanding officer saw me stir at that and frowned. "Well, you're doing well at your job, Roberts, and I don't want to lose you. But … if it's in the best interests of the country, I'd have let you go."

I glowed inside at her praise. "Thank you, Ma'am."

"You want me to put your name forward then?"

"Yes, please, Ma'am. If it turns out that they don't want me, I'll come back here."

F/O Marten nodded. "Get back to work, then."

Nothing happened for a week – except a huge storm that grounded all planes, ours and theirs, for a couple of days.

The afternoon flying resumed I spent staring at a few friendly blips on the RDF screen. At the end of my stint, I stood massaging my aching neck. "There's nothing happening, Betty," I told my relief, rubbing my ears, now free of the heavy headphones, and rotating my head to relieve the tension in my neck. "There's a couple of Spits up from Kirkwall and that's all."

She slipped into the seat and put on the headphones. "Okay."

I stepped away from the set and stretched, still working my neck to relieve the kinks.

Time for a tea.

The complete lack of drinkable coffee no longer disappointed me. I headed towards the kitchen but the F/O intercepted me.

"Ah, Roberts. Step into my office for a minute, please."

I followed her down the corridor into her office. "Shut the door, please and sit down."

Here we go again …

"Yes, Ma'am."

She sat at her desk and picked up a file. "It seems we're losing you after all."

"Er … yes, Ma'am?"

"You're being transferred to a station down south. You're to report to a Flight Lieutenant James at this address in London to pick up further orders." She scowled down at the file. "This is a bit irregular, but that's what the orders say."

Whatever.

"Yes, Ma'am."

"Here's your orders and a travel warrant. I suggest you get packed this evening and head out on tomorrow morning's ferry."

I took the proffered papers and, with a sigh, she picked up another file.

"I've now got to rearrange the shifts – yet again – to cover for your absence." She glanced up. "Off you go, then." Her voice betrayed resignation at this task.

"Yes, Ma'am."

Back outside, I met Sergeant Ackers in the kitchen. "I'm being transferred, Sarge."

"Oh yeah." She tilted an eyebrow at me. "Where to, you lucky girl?"

I shrugged. "Down south somewhere. I'm to report to some office in London to pick up the details."

"Really?" Sergeant Ackers sounded doubtful. "That's a bit unusual."

"The boss said that too." I thought for a moment. "Something about security, I suppose."

She laughed. "They're worried that Adolf might win the war if he finds out where you're going?"

"Of course." I joined her in laughing.

"Sorry to be losing you, Colette." She clapped me on the shoulder. "You're heading off tomorrow?"

"Yes, Sarge."

She glanced at the wall clock. "You're back on in half-an-hour for your final shift. Don't screw it up."

"No, Sarge." You needed to keep your wits about you on this job.

The rumour mill worked in high gear and by shift's end everyone in the watch knew about my transfer. A bit of a crowd gathered round me once we'd handed over. They congratulated me and called for drinks at the pub.

"Roberts." The boss's voice cut through the chatter.

All of a sudden, everyone remembered they needed to be doing something urgent, somewhere else and the crowd evaporated.

F/O Marten watched them scurry away, mastering a smile before turning back to me.

"Yes, Ma'am?"

"You're in luck. There's an Anson heading down to Linton-on-Ouse from Kirkwall tomorrow morning. If you report to the flight line before oh-nine-hundred hours you can catch a ride."

"Thank you, Ma'am."

She nodded and half turned away before speaking over her shoulder. "Don't stay long at the pub tonight. You want to catch that plane." She smiled. "Pass that on to your watch as well."

"Yes, Ma'am."

I went and cleared out my locker, struggled into the heavy but necessary greatcoat, then climbed into the back of the truck heading to our digs in Kirkwall.

"What'd the boss want?" Jane asked in her lilting Welsh accent.

"Seems like there's an Anson heading down to near York tomorrow morning and I can get a ride on it."

"There's luck for you. That'll save you a day, at least."

I smiled round at the dimly seen faces. "She also told me to tell you all to go easy at the pub tonight."

The watch muttered and groaned, but we all knew the price for turning up worse for wear. Everyone took their job seriously, even up here in the wilds of the Orkneys.

At the pub, I stood a round of shandies for the girls and we walked back to our digs by twenty-one-thirty, a bit buzzed, perhaps, but we'd be bright-eyed and bushy-tailed in the morning.

November 1940

I asked at the airfield guardhouse and they directed me to a hut where I'd find my pilot.

A man in flight gear glanced up from a chart spread on a table. "You're early." He growled.

"Sorry, sir." I gulped.

He saw my kitbag. "Not got the kitchen sink in there, I hope?"

"No sir." I lifted my bag in one hand, indicating it wasn't heavy.

He grunted and turned away to consult a different chart and I sat in a corner, trying to be unobtrusive.

About fifteen minutes later, the door banged, letting in another officer in flying gear with a gust of wind that lifted the charts, sending them twirling to the floor.

"Bloody hell."

"Language, Freddy. There's a lady present." The new officer made a half-embarrassed and half-amused face at me.

The pilot turned and scowled. He barely controlled himself, words slipping halfway off his tongue. "You're late, Pilot Officer Charles."

He retrieved the charts, folding them to show a heavy pencil line – our track, I supposed. With a glower at his co-pilot, he grabbed his flight bag and strode out of the door.

Pilot Officer Charles stared after him for a moment, one eyebrow quirked up, then turned to me. "Must've got out of bed the wrong side ... or something." He sighed. "Ah well, I'm sure we'll get you to where you need to be. Come on, Miss. We mustn't keep the boss waiting."

I hoisted my kitbag onto my shoulder and followed P/O Charles.

He watched me lift my kitbag. "Need a hand with that?"

"No sir, thank you sir."

We walked across to the Anson, parked on the apron with a couple of ground crew waiting nearby. The prospect of my first flight excited me. Once aboard, the two engines fired up and we bounced across the field. After running up the engines, creating a deafening noise, we turned into wind and took off. From my window, I watched the ground fall away as we headed out over the sea. Despite my excitement, the engines' drone seduced me into a doze. The change in engine noise as we neared our destination woke me and I watched the ground rise to meet us until we bumped across the grass, slowing and then turned towards the airfield buildings.

Once the engines shut down, the ringing in my ears persisted for hours. At the guardhouse, I found a truck headed for the main railway station in York to continue my journey south to London. I arrived at Kings Cross station well after midnight; we'd waited an hour to the north of the city for a raid to end. I'd watched the searchlights and Ack-Ack probing a sky lit by the fires on the ground, wondering how we might use radar to guide fighters against the bombers during the hours of darkness.

There had to be a way …

I found the station NAAFI cart. "A mug of tea and a sandwich, please."

"Here you go, love. You look beat – Navy, Army and Air Force Institute to the rescue, eh?"

I gave her a weary smile. "Thanks." I found a quiet corner and sat on the ground, munching on the sandwich washed down with strong NAAFI tea. I had to wait for the Underground to open in the morning – the best way to get to Baker Street as streets would be closed from the raid. I spent the rest of an uncomfortable night on the floor of Kings Cross station, bundled against a wall in my greatcoat, using my lumpy kitbag as a pillow.

Tired and bedraggled, I arrived at 64 Baker Street at zero eight thirty and searched for a sign on the building indicating an RAF office. Not finding one, I showed my papers to the army guard post. They inspected my documents and waved me inside.

"I have an appointment with Flight Lieutenant James." I told the reception desk – manned by a civilian.

What a strange RAF office.

She waved me to a row of chairs against a wall. "Take a seat."

I dropped my kitbag down beside a chair and sat. My eyelids drooped and I fought a losing battle to stay awake.

"Roberts?"

I jerked upright to find an army officer standing in front of me.

I stumbled to my feet and saluted. "Yes, sir." I felt myself swaying from a mix of fatigue and confusion.

Why army?

"Papers?" He held out his hand.

"Yes, sir." I dragged the now crumpled papers out of my greatcoat pocket and passed them over.

The officer examined them, his eyes inspecting me before handing them back. "Follow me." He strode off down a corridor.

I grabbed my kitbag and ran a couple of steps to catch up. We went along a dim corridor and then downstairs into a dingy office in the basement.

The officer indicated a chair and then sorted through a tray of files. He extracted one out of the pile and leafed through it. After a while he leaned back, speaking Parisian French. "How well do you know Paris?"

I felt my brain shift gears as I answered in the same language. "Quite well, I think. I lived there for about fifteen years."

As we talked, in French, it became clear that this officer knew Paris quite well.

"You have relatives in Normandy?"

I blinked in surprise at this. "Er ... Yes, sir. My aunt and cousins live near Caen ... or lived. Mother has still heard nothing from Aunt Evangeline. Two of her sons served in the French Army ..." I petered out and found myself giving a Gallic shrug.

"Are you enjoying your work with the RAF." He asked, switching back to English.

The sudden change of subject and language threw me for a moment. "Umm...yes, sir." I made an effort to concentrate through the fatigue-induced fog invading my head.

"Does that mean you want to continue doing that work?"

I tried to reach behind the words, to sense the direction he wanted to go, but nothing came to me, so I responded with care. "That depends, I think, sir."

The officer leaned back in his chair, steepling his fingers. "What do you mean?"

I tried to gather myself, realising that what I said might see me sent off to count spoons and forks at some remote base. "I think it depends, sir, on the other options."

The officer remained still, peering at me over his fingertips.

"We need people who speak French."

13

I squeezed my eyes shut, trying to force myself to think. "Doing what?" I opened my eyes and saw a frown forming. "Sir." I added. The incipient frown faded.

"Well now, I can't tell you that."

Was that a smile in his voice?

I frowned. "I beg your pardon? ... Sir?"

He leaned towards me. "Our job is top secret and dangerous." His brown eyes darkened as they scrutinised me, an assessment that became uncomfortable as the moment lengthened. Then he slid back in his seat, propping a foot nonchalantly on the edge of the desk. "If that interests you, come back tomorrow morning at eleven-thirty hours."

I cleared my throat, but he spoke over me. "There's a bed for you at this address." He flipped a slip of paper across to me. "If you decide not to join us, report to Flight Officer Swan at RAF Hatfield by sixteen-hundred hours tomorrow."

The paper held an address ... Flat 2, 16 Montagu Square.

The officer reached across, stripping the slip out of my fingers. "Off you go then, but not a word about this place or what we've discussed." He fixed me with a hard stare. "Not with anyone."

I sat there for a moment until he waved me away from his desk. "Go."

I stood up, my exhaustion warring with rising anger at his off-hand manner, anger that momentarily overpowered my fatigue and enabled a salute, sarcastic in its perfection. "Sir."

I should have saved the effort: his eyes remained on my file. I took a deep breath, picked up my kitbag and walked upstairs and out of the building. At that point I realised I needed directions to get to Montagu Square. I turned back to the guard. "Excuse me. How do I get to Montagu Square?"

The guard smiled. "Easy, Miss." He pointed up the street. "Go up Baker Street t' Dorset Street, turn lef' an' go 'til you find Mon'agu Square on your lef'." He sniffed. "'bout five min."

"Thank you."

Following his directions, I arrived at 16 Montagu Square – part of a long terrace of four-storey, white, stucco buildings. Sixteen offered an array of numbered bells. I pressed the one for 2. Nothing happened for a while, then I heard a shout from above me. I stepped back down the front steps. A woman with a towel wrapped round her head leaned out of a window.

"You rang number two?" She called down.

"Yes." I shouted back.

She scrutinised my RAF uniform. "Hang on, I'll toss you a key."

The woman disappeared for a moment.

"Here you go."

The key with a length of ribbon attached arced down and I managed to catch it.

She acknowledged my catch with a smile. "Come on up."

The ribbon carried two keys and one unlocked the front door. I dragged myself and my kitbag up two flights of stairs and found the door labelled 2. The second key opened that one. I walked into a room that stopped me with its elegance. A glass-fronted cabinet displaying delicate porcelain figurines stood opposite the door; armchairs with embroidered covers and antimacassars matched the rich carpet; a *chaise longue* with a tapestry rug rumpled across it nestled against the elegant brocade wallpaper and in the far corner stood a sideboard covered in various bottles and decanters.

A moment later, the woman reappeared wrapped in a silk robe and rubbing her hair with a towel.

"Come in. I'm Claire."

"Colette."

We shook hands and she smiled at my tousled appearance. "Fancy a bath?"

I shifted in my uniform, feeling the accumulated grime of my travels. "Yes, please."

Claire showed me into a bedroom with a large bed. "You can use this one." She pointed to a towel on the radiator. "The bathroom's just down on the left."

"Thanks."

I retrieved my dressing gown from the kitbag, undressed and headed into the bathroom clutching my dirty underwear. I yearned to fill the bath and luxuriate in hot water, but I kept to the five-inch rationing line.

Fifteen minutes later, clean and somewhat rejuvenated, I headed for my bedroom.

Claire heard me close the bathroom door, calling out, "Come down here and we'll have a gin. I think you need it."

15

"Just a mo." I headed into my room and draped my washed underwear over the radiator to dry.

I found Claire in her robe lounging on the *chaise*, her feet under the tapestry rug. My woollen dressing gown and slippers were dowdy in comparison.

She jumped up and clattered amongst the bottles. "Pink or a slice of lemon?"

"Sorry?"

She frowned. "Would you like a pink gin or just a slice of lemon?"

In France I'd drunk wine but a Leading Aircraft Woman's pay didn't stretch further than the occasional beer or shandy. "I've not drunk gin before."

"Hmmm ..." Her eyes assessed me. "Slice of lemon, I think." She turned back to the drinks table, clattering with bottles and glasses before handing me a tumbler in which a thin slice of lemon floated, aided by the bubbles appearing in the clear liquid.

"Sit yourself down and tell me what brings you here."

I sniffed the tumbler, smelling the alcohol, and took a cautious sip, enjoying its tartness. I took a bigger sip, savouring the unusual flavour as the officer's admonishment ran though my brain. "I'm being transferred – somewhere." I shrugged. "I'll find out tomorrow."

"But how did you end up here?" Claire's threw an arm out, sweeping round to indicate the elegant flat.

My mind raced. "When I turned up to collect my orders, they weren't ready as I arrived earlier than expected and they bundled me off here." I gave Claire an embarrassed smile. "I spent the night sleeping on the floor in Kings Cross station."

Claire nodded in sympathy. "Is that a French accent I can hear?"

Uh ... oh ...

"I'm English."

"Hmm...Colette. That's a French name."

My eyes narrowed. "Why all the questions?"

"Sorry, sorry. Just my insatiable curiosity." She saw my half-empty glass. "Drink up. I'll make you another."

I felt the alcohol combining with my fatigue. "No thanks. I'm headed for some shuteye."

"Okay." It was drawn out, speculative. "I'll wake you in time for dinner?"

"Thanks."

I drained my glass, handed it back to Claire and headed into my room.

***

Claire cooked vegetables and a meat pie for dinner, the filling of an indeterminate, chewy origin. We drank half a bottle of red wine, which helped. Once again, Claire kept probing me and I kept deflecting her.

After a while I got sick of it. "Claire, they drummed into us in basic to keep our mouths shut ... loose lips sink ships, and all that."

Claire's eyes were devoid of any embarrassment.

I glared across the table. "You can keep asking me questions, but I'm not telling you anything about me or what I do." We exchanged stares across the table.

The silence stretched and I searched for something to say. "Why don't you tell me about yourself." I looked around at the flat. "How come you're living in such a posh place?"

Claire's eyes held mine for a moment. Then she leaned back in her chair, sighing and looking round as if viewing the flat and its contents for the first time. "Is it posh?" She murmured. "Well, it's not my flat. It's Daddy's." Her face dropped. "The Germans captured him fighting in the rear-guard at Dunkirk. He's in a POW camp, somewhere in Germany, but at least he's alive."

I saw the pain in her eyes and stayed silent.

Her lips pursed, tasting the remembered worry. "For over a month, we heard nothing then notification came through the Red Cross." Her eyes returned to me and her voice firmed. "I work as a secretary for the government." She glanced around the room. "This flat's too rich for my pay."

I wondered where Daddy's money came from to own such a place but realised if I started probing, Claire could start questioning me again.

I stood up. "Let me wash up since you cooked."

Claire smiled. "Okay – but I'll dry up and put away – you don't know where things go."

We finished in ten minutes and I yawned.

"I think I'll go to bed, Claire."

"Fair enough. I leave for work in the morning at about half-past seven. What time do you report?"

"Not until eleven-thirty."

"Lucky you – lie in and make a cup of tea. When you leave, drop the keys into two's letterbox."

"Okay – goodnight – and thanks for the bed."

"Sleep well."

Claire settled back onto the *chaise longue* with a book as I headed to my room. I lay in bed trying to decide if something 'top secret and dangerous' attracted me. It sounded scary and exciting at the same time.

November – December 1940

Claire had already left when I roused myself. I pottered around, made a cup of tea and sat in the kitchen in my dressing gown and slippers, trying to decide what to do. Being alone in Claire's flat made me feel uncomfortable so I dressed in my uniform, packed up and headed out. A long, narrow park filled the centre of Montagu Square, overlooked by the tall houses on both sides of the street. I wandered into this, found a bench seat, parked my kitbag at one end and leaned back against it.

As I'd dropped off to sleep, the adventurous side of me had edged towards accepting the offer of a secret and dangerous job. In the cold light of a dingy November morning, I thought about my RDF work. According to F/O Marten at Nether Button, as a skilled operator I contributed to the war effort. But I had joined up wanting to help liberate France; if this work needed French speakers, then its help must be greater.

Mustn't it?

After quite a long time of pondering this, the dingy sky pockmarked with barrage balloons produced a fine drizzle, so I stood, grabbed my kitbag and headed back to 64 Baker Street. I'd be early but I hoped to wait there in the dry.

Outside, I showed my orders to the guard and went in. The receptionist inspected me.

"Back again?"

"Yes. I need to see Flight Lieutenant James, please."

Or whatever he's calling himself today...

As before, they told me to sit and wait. I sat for about thirty minutes, but this time I saw the officer coming, stood up and saluted.

"Follow me, Roberts."

We trod the same route down into his basement office, where he again sat and consulted a file. After a minute he placed the file on the table and opened a cigarette case, leaning across to offer me one. "Cigarette?"

"No, thank you, sir."

He lit his and inhaled deeply, sighing out a long feather of smoke. "So, you want to join our madcap band of lunatics?"

"Sir?"

"What we're doing is dangerous. You must be mad if you want to join us." His eyes narrowed watching me as he drew on his cigarette.

I swallowed.

Was this part of assessing me?

"Everything in war is dangerous, so I don't think I'm mad, sir." I stared back across the desk. "I want to help France."

His eyes held mine, smoke dribbling from his nose. "Hmm." His face signalled his approval. "Well, you know how to keep your mouth shut."

What?

He sat forward. "Go to office twelve, up on the second floor. They'll get you started."

I stood up and saluted. "Yes, sir."

I headed upstairs with my kitbag. I passed closed doors with typewriters clacking behind them. When I found room 12, its closed door also concealed a typewriter. I knocked firmly to be heard above the noise.

The clacking continued but a female voice called out, "Come in."

I opened the door and jerked to a stop, just managing to hang on to my kitbag: Claire. I'd been set up: she'd been told to watch me and report.

"Welcome, Colette. Congratulations ..." Her smile of welcome quirked oddly. "... if that's the right word."

I stood there, confused.

"Come in, I'll get you squared away." She smiled but it felt ... distant. "First of all, there's a bathroom two doors down the corridor on the left. Go and change into civvies."

Ten minutes later back in Claire's office, she smiled again, perhaps recognising the French cut of my clothes, though creased from days in my kitbag.

Claire pointed to a set of forms on her desk. "Sign these forms, please."

I glanced at them. "I've already signed the Official Secrets Act – when I joined the WAAFs."

Claire stared back at me. "Sign them again, please."

I shrugged and signed them. Claire gathered them up and put them in a file.

"You'll start your training at Wanborough Manor, near Guildford." She handed me a one-pound note and a docket to sign.

"Umm ..."

"We don't use travel warrants – you're a civilian." Her eyes revealed nothing. "You'll need to account for every penny and give back any change when you get to Wanborough."

I nodded, feeling a bit odd at being a civilian again. "Am I out of the WAAFs then?"

Claire's face remained blank. "No – you're still a WAAF and still subject to military discipline. But you're on detached duty where you're a civilian as far as everyone is concerned."

Okay.

Claire went on. "Get yourself to Waterloo station and on to the train to Guildford. A George Fredericks will meet you. You're called Veronica Cheeseworth."

I blinked in confusion.

Claire just stared back. "No real names."

I swallowed, the implications of my decision becoming clearer. "Okay."

Civilian clothes felt strange after months in uniform, but I carried a service kitbag and that combination attracted a couple of curious stares. During the ride to Guildford, I thought about what happened with Claire at her flat: it had been a test.

This meeting at the station will be a test too – and so warranted some thought.

At Guildford station, I walked down the platform and into the station building, searching unobtrusively for a George Fredericks – whatever that might be. I positioned myself on a bench seat outside, keeping a surreptitious eye on the surroundings with the help of the mirror in my powder compact as I dabbed at my makeup. After about five minutes a man walked nervously up the street and sat down beside me.

"Welcome, Veronica." He tried to sound confident, but his hands were trembling.

I shifted away from him and turned. "I beg your pardon?"

The man blushed at my supercilious tone. "Oh, I'm sorry, Miss. My mistake." He jumped to his feet.

"That depends."

He stopped. "Veronica Cheeseworth?"

"And you are?" I fixed him with the same gimlet stare my French grandmother used when her servants displeased her.

His eyes wandered, unsure of himself. "Ummm ... I'm ... er ... George Fredericks."

I stood up. "Well, come along then."

He stood there, blinking. "You're Veronica Cheeseworth?"

I held my austere gaze then nodded, once.

"Oh, thank goodness. I thought I'd stuffed up this exercise too." He stood, motionless, thoroughly flustered.

I raised an eyebrow. "Well?"

"Oh ... yes. Come with me."

We set off and turned into a side street where he opened the boot of a large car and I deposited my kitbag inside. He ushered me into the backseat, seating himself in the front passenger seat.

After a moment, another man slid in through the far rear door and sat down beside me. He tapped the driver on the shoulder. "Back to base."

"Yes, sir."

The man smacked 'George Fredericks' on the shoulder. "She made mincemeat of you, didn't she?"

'George' half-turned, his demeanour sheepish. "Well, ... perhaps ... a bit."

The man beside me shook his head and turned to me. "Welcome, Veronica." He leaned back into the corner, surveying me and smiling to himself. "I think we can make something of you."

I managed to stop myself from replying and tried to keep my face neutral despite the uncertainty bubbling within me. Then he turned to the window and the rest of the journey passed in silence until we arrived in front of a large house with nearby outbuildings – presumably Wanborough Manor.

"Okay George. Take Veronica up to room eight." He turned to me. "Get settled in this afternoon. We'll start you off in the morning."

I grabbed my kitbag from the boot and followed George into the grand interior and up two flights of stairs. George pointed down a corridor. "Eight's down there – on the left I think."

"Thanks ..."

He turned away.

"George, I hope I didn't get you into trouble at the station?"

He turned back, sighing. "I'm not sure I'm cut out for this caper." Uncertainty quivered on his face. "Every day I think they'll wash me out ... it'll happen soon, I'm sure."

I had no idea what to say, so I smiled a goodbye and walked down the corridor, searching for room eight. I found it at the end. My knock went unanswered so I went in. The ceiling sloped and two standard barrack beds with their lockers stood either side of a gable window. Both were unmade but held a neat stack of bedclothes. A cupboard sporting a couple of coat hangers completed the basic furnishings.

I sat on one of the beds, bouncing it to assess its comfort – it was satisfactory. I unpacked my kitbag into the cupboard and made the bed. Task complete, I went to the window.

Gunfire?

I struggled for a moment with the stiff latch before the sound of gunfire became clear through the open window – shots and short bursts coming from behind the woods across a field. The realisation that I would learn to fire guns both excited and scared me.

I stood there listening until the gunfire stopped. Some minutes later, a group of eight people, including two women, appeared from the woods, some of them with rifles slung from their shoulder or cradling some sort of tommy gun in their arms. They laughed amongst themselves until they disappeared round the house.

Time for me to explore.

Downstairs, I heard voices coming from the back of the house and so explored through a dining room into the kitchen and scullery. Through a window I saw the group sitting on the ground, pulling their weapons apart on a canvas groundsheet.

I dithered for a minute until one of the men noticed me and waved me outside.

His eyes raked me up and down, raising an eyebrow at my smart clothes before turning to one of the women. "'Ere, Dolly. Show this girl 'ow to strip an' clean a Sten."

One of the women cast a baleful eye at the man but gestured me over. She waved at my smart dress. "You'll want to find some clothes you don't care about." She wore tweed slacks, showing various stains and a jumper that had seen better days. She wiped a vagrant lock of her brown hair out of her eyes, depositing a smear of gun oil on her forehead. "I'm Susan."

She saw my confusion and huffed. "He'll come up with a nickname for you too ... he thinks it's funny, I suppose." She patted the canvas, inviting me to kneel beside her on the edge of the sheet. "What's your name?"

"Ummm ... Veronica."

Susan laughed. "You've just arrived?"

I nodded.

"You can use your real name here, not the one for the play acting at the station."

"Gerron wiv it, Dolly."

Susan rolled her eyes. "Yes, Sarge."

She gestured down at the Sten. "Seen one of these before?"

I shook my head. "No ... I'm Colette."

Susan nodded and then proceeded to strip down the Sten, explaining as she went. She grabbed a rag and a pull-through from the centre of the canvas, oiling and cleaning the parts. Then it all went back together at speed. She waved to attract the sergeant's attention. "Done, Sarge."

"Okay Dolly, you can fall out." He winked across at me. "See ya tomorrer, Frenchie."

I raised an eyebrow.

Susan chuckled. "Come on, Frenchie." She stood up, wiping her hands on a rag she tossed back onto the canvas. "I stink of cordite or whatever they use in the cartridges." Her nose wrinkled in distaste. "*Parfum du jour* in a war, I suppose, but I prefer Chanel. I'm heading to a bath then I'll show you around before dinner."

I followed Susan inside.

"Meet you back in the hall in twenty minutes?"

"Okay."

I wandered back through the house and sat in one of the leather button-back chairs in the hall.

Would I ever be that confident and competent with a gun?

I mulled that idea for a while before concluding that training with guns meant certain travel to occupied France. The implications of 'secret and dangerous' sank in further and my stomach fluttered.

24

Winter darkness had engulfed the manor by the time Susan reappeared, so we toured the inside of the house – classrooms, toilets, offices. At one point we passed a door marked *Major de Wesselow*.

"That's the CO – you'll get called in there but once."

"And?"

"You've either passed initial selection or RTU – returned to unit." Susan's eyes were thoughtful as she surveyed me. "What lot are you in?"

"The WAAFs."

"Good for you." She smiled. "I'm a Land Girl and I don't want to go back to scrabbling potatoes out of the mud again." She shuddered at the memory.

At dinner, the other woman – Gladys – joined us. She shared a room with Susan.

"You're lucky, having a room to yourself." Gladys remarked, sniffing to indicate the luck was undeserved. "Anyway, that will end as soon as they send down another woman."

I shrugged. After my experiences in the WAAFs, sharing a room no longer held any terrors for me. At the end of the meal, Gladys bid us both goodnight, admonishing Susan not to wake her when she came to bed.

Susan watched her out of earshot. "She's so prim and proper I can't see her surviving here."

"I'm heading for bed too. I've had an exhausting couple of days getting here and need to catch up on my sleep."

She nodded. "Okay. But set your alarm for six tomorrow morning. Physical jerks start in the courtyard at half past and they're hard on anyone late."

The three weeks at Wanborough were an exhausting mix of physical exercise, orienteering in the surrounding winter countryside and classroom activities. Apart from learning to shoot, I also learned the basics of using explosives, participated in intense interrogation, on both sides of the table, and started learning morse code. A handful of people washed out (including George – his real name, apparently – and Gladys), but we didn't talk about that – 'bad form' it turns out.

I organised a parcel of clothes from home as I had few civilian clothes with me. I tried to use some of my uniform for the dirtiest jobs but received discouraging comments – 'bad form' again. From a phone box during an orienteering exercise on day two, I spoke to my mother and told her that I needed working clothes, stout shoes and a suitcase. Some of my things arrived – but my mother (perhaps with help from granny Roberts) had put together a package that owed something, I suspect, to the Red Cross donations that came in for the evacuated children: being small had its advantages.

Late in the third week they bundled a group of us into the back of a truck and dropped us off one by one on the South Downs. We had to find our way to a place called Broad Hinton about fifteen miles distant before sunset without getting picked up by the police, who were alert to our presence. This was not an easy task as the signposts were gone, removed to make it difficult for the *Boche* if they invaded. But Wanborough did provide us with a sketch map.

I'd scavenged some bread and cheese at breakfast as the rumour mill told of a planned exercise, so I had something to keep me from starving and fortune smiled on us with cold but dry weather. We had to go through – or round – Marlborough. Thinking about it, I expected the police to concentrate there. I decided to skirt round the eastern side of the town, staying in the country – and it worked like a charm. I walked into Broad Hinton in just over five and a half hours, never having seen a policeman. I'm sure the walks I'd taken with the evacuees in and around the New Forest had helped me read the countryside. A mug of tea and a doorstop of a meat paste sandwich appeared as I waited for everyone else.

About half of us had arrived two hours later and they took us back to Wanborough in a truck. The dining room that night had gaps: the police kept the people they caught in the cells overnight.

At breakfast, one of the instructors tapped me on the shoulder. "Report to Major de Wesselow, Colette."

Nerves jangling, I knocked on the CO's door.

"Come."

"LAC Roberts reporting as requested, sir." I managed not to salute, not being in uniform, but I was automatically at attention.

"Ah yes, our little French girl."

I squirmed ... it was dismissive and demeaning. I assumed I was RTU and my stomach sank but a hidden tension released.

He searched through a stack of files on his desk until he found the one he wanted. "Stand easy."

I relaxed from attention and watched his face as he scanned my file.

"The RAF think quite highly of you and they'd like you back."

I swallowed my disappointment.

Had my father decided this was too dangerous for his darling daughter and pulled some strings to get me out?

The major flipped a couple of pages.

"Well, Roberts, it's their loss. We're going to keep you."

His voice reached me from a distance and it took a moment to register. I let out a breath – softly.

I'd made it.

And that tension returned.

"Someone with your recent experience of France will help make life difficult for Adolf and his friends."

He tossed the file into his out basket. "Get yourself to the office and they'll arrange transport for you to Scotland."

"Yes sir."

His gaze held me for a moment, his face neutral. "Good luck. You'll need it."

I nodded, snapping to attention. "Sir," suppressing the urge to salute. As I closed the door, the impact of his words prickled my scalp and energised the flutter in my stomach.

The office had my travel papers drawn up – for Airsaig in Scotland. I packed up all my WAAF service gear into my kitbag – civilian gear only from now on. The office undertook to send the kitbag to my grandparent's house.

Within a couple of hours, I sat at Guildford station about to head north. With the disruption of the Blitz, the journey took three interminable, uncomfortable, sleep-interrupted days and nights. I arrived at Fort William dishevelled and groggy with fatigue, trying to find the train to Airsaig.

"Weel, lassie. Ye's in luck. 'Tis o'er there." The porter waved at three carriages attached behind a gently steaming engine.

With my suitcase dragging down my arm, I clambered into one of the carriages, tucked myself into a corner seat, closed my eyes and snoozed.

December 1940 – November 1941

That set a definite trend: the weeks I spent at Airsaig were marked by insufficient sleep. At every opportunity I wedged myself into some corner and catnapped. After the regular morning physical jerks and runs at Wanborough, I thought I was fit – but a day at Airsaig proved me wrong. By the end of the first week, I had blisters on my feet together with scrapes on my knees, elbows and hands from the scrambling in and around the rocky hills and along the coast as we raced to complete another obstacle course. They followed these 'races' with a session of personal combat – with a knife or unarmed. I learned that, in spite of my small size and light weight, I could – sometimes – win against larger opponents. And for me, everyone was larger.

Christmas came and went ... and then New Year.

I learned about British and some German weapons – shooting them, stripping, cleaning and reassembling them blindfold. I was no crack shot, but I learned to hit the target with whatever weapon given me. Always the emphasis was on pointing the weapon and the 'double tap' – two shots with a pistol or two quick bursts with the Sten or equivalent. We also trained with explosives. Despite the risk of blowing myself up, I found this fascinating. I had a knack for assessing the smallest amount of explosive set in the perfect place to drop a telegraph pole or destroy a rail line. It pleased some strange, internal aesthetic and the explosions satisfied an unexpected destructive urge. But even with all the training, I remained uncertain about killing anyone with a gun and had a nightmare about trying to kill with a knife.

Could I do this?

Days blurred together – until the interrogations started. Classes had discussed withstanding interrogation, but we learned the ugly truth that almost everyone breaks. We had to convince the interrogation team that we couldn't be broken before they succeeded in doing so – or break in such a way that they believed the rubbish information we spilled.

Implied was the execution following either outcome. Stories circulated in whispers about agents who had disappeared into the Nazi's maw ...

My uncertainty increased and fear – of failure, of lack of courage – grew inside me.

Then we went 'in the cage' for real. Despite the sleep deprivation, humiliation and physical abuse, I wondered if they treated me gentler than the men. A small miracle happened during the process – I detached from my body; I could see everything they did, but it didn't matter, even when half-suffocated by a wet cloth over my face or left naked, wet and shivering in isolation.

After three intense weeks at Airsaig they sent me off to learn about operating a radio behind enemy lines – reading and sending Morse at ever higher speeds, codes and cyphers, radio fault finding and repair. We had to pick – or create – a short poem and commit it to memory. That was the basis of our coding scheme. I chose Verlaine's *Song of Autumn* – in French, which I'd learned in school: I felt its tortured melancholy suited the purpose. This caused a bit of a stir as they weren't used to foreign language poems, but they allowed it after a discussion.

All the while, the physical fitness regime continued with time on the firing range. As the end of the course approached, the tension rose amongst us: the time approached for us to go to France and my self-doubt deepened.

When the course finished, I was told to report to Bletchley Park. Everyone else headed to Manchester for parachute training. I was not going to France.

What had I done wrong? Had they smelt my fear?

Bottling up my tears, I knocked on the CO's door.

The captain glanced up from the papers on his desk. "Yes?"

"Sir ... please, why aren't I going on to parachute training?"

"Umm ... Roberts?"

Yes sir."

He surveyed a stack of files in his out tray and then back at me. "Roberts ... let me assure you that you passed the course." He smiled. "Your performance rated excellent in every part of the training."

I stared at my feet in confused, dejected silence before looking up. "So, why didn't they send me to the parachute training?"

The captain shrugged. "I don't know." He glanced again at the files in his out tray. "When I reported the list of passing students, they posted you all to parachute training. But then a signal came through instead posting you to ... er ..." He turned a questioning face towards me.

"Bletchley Park, sir."

"Ah yes, quite so, Bletchley Park."

"But ... why, sir?"

"I have no idea, LAC Roberts, because I don't need to know." I heard the exasperation in his voice. "Your job is to shut up and get on with it." His eyes fell to the papers spread on his desk. "Dismissed."

I came to attention. "Sir."

The two-day journey south allowed me to examine my emotions, swirling around a deep, personal shame. Not heading to France had removed the fear and replaced it with shame. Deserting my companions and abandoning my desire to help France fuelled that shame into a greasy flame that blistered and charred without consuming. It scorched my psyche.

I heard but ignored the voice that argued it was not my choice, others had decided not to send me: but I knew my courage had failed; I'd failed France.

Two days later, I found myself in the Security Intelligence Service radio section at Bletchley Park, helping run the British side of the communications with agents in Europe – people doing the job I was supposed to do. I was back in uniform, billeted in the nearby village. I received coded Morse messages from our agents in Europe and sent coded messages to them. I knew how to create such messages from poem codes and I occupied part of my mind trying to work out the poems in use, without success.

However deep my concentration on the job, my guilt and shame remained: a continuous, souring presence, a constant reminder of my failure. When a callsign went silent, I felt it as a searing stab to my conscience: another agent killed or captured, possibly one of my group, who had done what I could not. Being promoted corporal in August rubbed salt into these open sores: if people knew me, they'd kick me out, not promote me.

I rebuffed approaches from interested men, increasingly morose in my self-imposed isolation. We had little private time and my darkening mood scared off further attempts at friendship. My sleep was broken, sliced asunder by guilt-ridden dreams – or nightmares.

I ran through the surrounding woods and fields every day and that helped – exhaustion and the rhythms encouraged sleep as well as preserving my fitness. But by autumn 1941 I had a serious problem; nights of broken sleep depleted my concentration and I feared making disastrous mistakes in a coded message. Furious concentration was the sole solution I had.

At the end November 1941, I dragged in for my evening shift as the thin, wintry light fled the sky to be ordered to my section commander's office. This was Mr Morris, supposedly a civilian but with SIS personnel, you never knew. I always called him 'sir' and stood to attention when I talked to him. I knocked on the door jamb.

"Come in corporal. Shut the door, please."

I closed it and stood at attention in front of his desk.

Had I cocked-up a message?

I tasted the bitterness of this different failure in my throat and waited for the axe to fall.

"Relax, corporal. Take a seat." He gestured to a chair to one side of his desk. I moved it and perched on the edge across from him, tension in every muscle.

He flipped through a file propped against the edge of the desk. "You were an RDF operator before ... well before this?"

I frowned in surprise. "Yes, sir."

He closed the file. "How do you feel about going back onto ops?"

I have cocked something up. They're kicking me back to the WAAFs.

I sat there, numbed into silence.

Mr Morris didn't notice my reaction – he had his nose back in the file. "Your background is perfect for an urgent operation in France."

France ...

A spark of ... something ... kindled beneath the shame and guilt. "Sir?" My voice a surprised squeak.

Mr Morris stared at me over his glasses. "Your RDF background is a distinct bonus in this case and you've done all the SOE training."

"Not quite all, sir. I haven't done the parachute part."

Why did I say that? Shut up you idiot.

"That's easily arranged." His hand waved dismissively and he leaned back tipping his chair. "We'd like you to volunteer for this mission. Will you go?"

Fear clenched my stomach, but if I chickened out, that'd be the end of me. "Yes, sir." I swallowed, an acrid taste in my throat; that older fear had replaced my guilt and shame.

His chair swung upright. "Well, I'm sorry to lose you but our Special Operations Executive friends insist they need you."

I heard the distaste in his voice at 'friends'; SIS and SOE competed for attention and funding. SIS made it clear they thought SOE were a bunch of bumbling amateurs fouling their patch.

"Get yourself to the admin office and pick up your orders."

I stood up. "Sir."

The following day, I stood outside 64 Baker Street, suitcase in hand, having my papers checked before entering. The guard showed no interest that I was wearing civvies.

November 1941 – December 1941

After reporting at the front desk, I found a seat where I had waited before. This time a civilian walked towards me. I jumped to my feet and turned my instinctive salute into an awkward, waist high wave. Amusement flashed across the man's face.

"Miss Roberts?"

"Yes, sir."

"Come with me please."

This time we went to a set of offices on the ground floor labelled "Section F".

"Have a seat." He waved at a chair as he sat behind his desk, picking up a file.

Mine?

Parisian-accented French flowed from him. "We urgently need to get you through some refresher training and off to France as soon as possible."

I felt my brain shift gears; it had been a year since I'd spoken French. A frisson ran across my skin, prickling my scalp.

"Where do I go for this retraining?"

"You'll stay here for about a week." He turned a few pages in the file. "Hmm … no parachute training."

"No, sir."

His eyes wandered, refocusing after a moment and continuing in English. "Well, I don't think you'll need it for this operation." He scribbled a note on a memo pad. "We'll fly you across in a Lysander."

I'd never heard of a Lysander, but it must be able to land in a field.

"Report here in the morning at oh-eight hundred. I'll get a pass for you tomorrow." He scribbled on a slip of paper. "For now, go up to office twelve."

"Yes, sir."

I picked up my suitcase and went upstairs to find Claire still in office twelve. She handed me a file and told me to take a seat until she finished work. The file reviewed SOE tradecraft – the skills and techniques of espionage. It also had a lengthy briefing section on the situation as we understood it in France in terms of ration cards, travel zones, permits and such.

I spent a week staying with Claire each night and in various parts of Section F during the long days, refreshing my trade craft and learning how to live in occupied France in 1941. Then they bundled me off to RAF Tempsford.

On my first day there I met with an unnamed, studious, man who spent an hour talking with me about my RDF days, probing my understanding of the equipment I had used and the techniques associated with using it. Helped by his gentle questions, I recalled a surprising amount. This man knew a great deal about RDF and I wondered about the purpose behind our meeting. After lunch, a Wing Commander briefed me on the utmost secrecy of everything I heard. He also told me that I was now confined to the station.

Back in the earlier room, the man returned – still no name – and showed me a pair of aerial photographs of a piece of equipment sitting in a field in front of a large house. It looked a bit like a concave dustbin lid.

A parabolic or spherical reflector?

As I picked up the photos, he asked. "Any idea what that might be?"

After inspecting the photograph for about half a minute, while recalling our earlier conversation, I raised an uncertain eyebrow. "A German RDF?"

The man's eyes showed approval, then his face dropped. "The Germans are shooting our bombers out of the sky in shocking numbers and we ... think ... it's due to improved German RDF – specifically a system that combines long-range and short-range systems to guide their night fighters and flak onto our bombers. We understand their long-range radar but this," he tapped the dustbin lid apparatus in one of the photos, "this is new and we need to understand how it works. Then we can block it or trick it."

The photograph, taken from a plane flying at low level, drew my attention for a moment. "How can I help?"

"I don't know." He shook his head with an exasperated sigh. "We can't keep losing bombers at this rate. We think this," he tapped the photo again, "is the reason but we need more information ..." He leant back in his seat eyeing me warily. "And I have no idea how you can help with that."

If he hadn't been briefed about me, he had no need to know, but I had to understand what he wanted. "What would help you counter this system?"

His eyes narrowed, his lips pursed and then he let out an explosive breath. "I want one of those sets in front of me, to take apart, test and understand." His shoulders slumped. "But I don't know how that's possible."

I kept my face blank: my mission would centre on helping to acquire this new RDF system. He stared at me for several seconds before he pushed his chair back, gathered up the photos into a file and left the room. I sat, wondering about what came next.

A minute later an RAF Flight Sergeant strode into the room. "Right 'o, Miss. Come wiv me, please."

He took me out of the building into the grey December afternoon. We walked for about five minutes, arriving at a firing range. He laid out on a canvas sheet a service revolver, a Sten and what looked like a German officer's pistol. I'd seen but not handled one at Airsaig.

"Okay Miss. Strip, check and reassemble these weapons."

I stripped and cleaned the service revolver but when I stripped the Sten, I found the firing pin was missing. "Umm, Sarge, the firing pin's missing from this."

His face remained blank but he reached into his pocket and tossed me the missing item. I cleaned and reassembled the weapon and then turned to the pistol. It had German writing on it. I found the safety and then the magazine ejection – it was empty, but there might be a round in the chamber. I pulled back the slide, ejecting a round.

The sergeant nodded his approval. "Ok miss – you can shoot that if you 'ave to." From a webbing bag he produced a magazine for the sten. "See if you can 'it the twen'y-five-yard target."

At least some of the rounds in the two bursts had made holes on the target. I scored better at the ten-yard target.

The sergeant produced some pistol rounds from the bag. "Now try the service revolver at ten yards."

I loaded the pistol and fired two rounds in the 'double tap' taught in my training.

The sergeant nodded in approval – both had hit the target. "Now at twenty-five yards."

I double-tapped again – one round in the target this time and repeated the effort with the German pistol with the same result.

He pointed at the weapons. "Unload and clean them."

I stripped and cleaned the Sten and service pistol. "How do I strip this, Sarge?" I pointed at the German pistol.

"Fair enough, miss. You'll do." He knelt beside me, stripping, cleaning and reassembling the pistol with quick, competent movements that I tried to file away. He put the remaining rounds and magazines in the webbing bag along with the pistols, hitching the Sten over his shoulder with the sling. "Follow me."

He walked me back to the building I'd spent the morning in for an afternoon being grilled about ID papers, travel passes and ration cards in occupied France.

In the morning, I refreshed my explosives skills behind an earth bank on the far side of the airfield. After half a day of scrabbling about in the winter mud setting charges, I wanted a hot bath. Back in my room I grabbed a towel and my faithful dressing gown. I washed myself in the permitted five inches of water – lying back in a full, hot bath was a distant, sybaritic memory.

I heard boots walk into the building. I sat up, wondering what was going on. Then the door burst open and arms dragged me out dripping wet, a hand clamped over my mouth stifling my scream. They carried me, naked except for a towel over my head, to a nearby building.

I was kept naked without sleep – but I was usually wet and cold, so I doubt I could have slept. Every few hours they tied me to a chair and slapped a wet flannel over my face, suffocating me, shouting at me to tell them about our RDF. After a while, I drifted out of my body to watch my interrogators' actions, detached from reality.

Finally, they took me back to my room and dumped me in a warm bath.

"Get cleaned up and sleep."

***

I woke in my bed and lay there, trying to reconstruct if I'd revealed anything during the mock interrogation before falling asleep again.

"Tea, Miss?" A WAAF stood beside my bed.

"Yes, please."

She placed the steaming mug on the locker. "Drink this and then come over to the office. They've got some lunch for you there."

I blinked. "What's the time?"

"Just gone twelve hundred hours, Miss." The WAAF smiled. "Enjoy your tea."

"Thank you."

I sat up with an embarrassed shiver, wrapping the bedclothes round me to cover my nakedness.

How many people had seen me naked during the interrogation?

I sipped the hot, sweet tea – unusually sweet, I realised, glad the sugar wasn't coming out of my ration. Sitting there, I knew I'd managed to drift away from my body during the interrogation here as I had at Airsaig. If captured, perhaps I'd weather the storm of interrogation that preceded the inevitable execution. The room shrank and darkened ...

Enough of the morbid thoughts.

Fifteen minutes later I stood at attention in front of the unnamed Wing Commander – the office doors lacked the usual name plates.

"Ah ... Roberts." His eyes shifted, unable to engage mine. "Are you ... um ... well?" His nervous fingers rolled a pencil to and fro.

"Yes, thank you, sir, now I've caught up on my sleep." My bright voice startled him and he dropped the pencil. It rolled towards me and off the desk, ending up at my feet. I picked it up and placed it in front of him.

His unease at what they had put me through filled his eyes when they met mine. "Umm ... thank you ... er ... sit down, Roberts."

I hesitated for a moment before sitting on the same model chair they had strapped me to during the interrogation. The Wing Commander had his eyes on the file in front of him – presumably my file.

"It appears that you're ..." He stumbled for a moment before continuing. "Er ... now ready.

I nodded, searching his face for any clue to my mission.

He sniffed. "There's still some unease about sending you off to France, given your knowledge of our RDF, even if it is now mostly out of date."

That was why I'd not gone on to the parachute training – they deemed my knowledge a security risk in France.

Part of the knot of self-doubt unclenched.

"Roberts?"

I had frozen for a moment and his worry about my recent treatment re-surfaced in his eyes. "Yes, sir." My smile was confident, masking the underlying tension.

His eyes narrowed as he looked me over.

Was he wondering if I was fit to go?

"I'm fine sir." I smiled again, trying to reassure him. "I've just realised why I didn't complete the parachute training before." My voice sought to soothe his concern. "They worried I might give away RDF secrets under interrogation if I were captured."

The Wing Commander's eyes widened for a moment. "Well ... um ...that's as maybe." He cleared his throat and his eyes dropped to the file before rising back to mine for reflective seconds. Then he snapped the file shut. "Go through that door, please." He pointed across the room.

As I stood up, he beat me to the door. "Good luck, Roberts." He nodded and then opened it for me.

A Wing Commander doing that for a lowly corporal flustered me. "Er ... thank you, sir."

I walked through the door and he closed it behind me.

"Good afternoon, Colette." Maurice Buckmaster, the head of section F greeted me.

I blinked. "Good afternoon, sir."

"Come over here." He indicated a table that held a large photomosaic stitched together from a dozen or more aerial photographs. It showed a piece of cliff-edged coastline, a small town on a sea-front and, set back from the cliffs, a house with the *Boche* RDF dish in front of it.

"This is Bruneval, where there's one of the short-range RDF sets. We want to nip in and steal it, but ..." He indicated some buildings at some distance from the house. "These are new and possibly the barracks of a defence force. Bunkers guard the beach with troops in another barracks above the town." His hand swept across the mosaic. "We need to know the size and quality of these forces, how they're organised and the size, distance, reaction time and quality of the inevitable reinforcements."

He leant back from the table. "We want you to link up with the local resistance, get them to find all this out and radio the information back to us."

I nodded.

Mr Buckmaster eyes held a fierce intensity. "We want not just the numbers of troops, but their unit or some indication of the quality of the forces ... and their commander, if possible."

"Understood, sir."

Mr Buckmaster pursed his lips, sucking in a breath. "We need that information as soon as you can get it. Once you've sent it, you will need to keep a close watch on things. If anything changes, anything at all, then you need to alert us – without delay."

I nodded.

He sat for a moment and I saw a moment of doubt on his face. "You've had all the training, but I must remind you not to get involved in any ... activity ... with the Maquis, the resistance." His face hardened. "You are not to risk capture. Tell them what we want, wait for them to get the information and then send it to us when they bring it to you."

"Understood, sir."

"Your codename is Marie and your contact's codename is Colonel Rémy." He waved at the photomosaic. "Learn the area. We'll fly you and your radio across in a day or two."

I jumped to my feet as Mr Buckmaster stood up. "Yes, sir." And he walked out of the room. I moved across to the table and started committing the photomosaic to memory.

I spent two days doing this, along with practicing coding/decoding messages with my poem code and learning the ins and outs of my radio, a different model to the one I'd trained on. I also learned how to get in and out of a Lysander with my radio and my personal bag.

After liaison with France, my insertion would happen the night of 10th and 11th December, a night with enough moonlight for navigation. During the final day I assembled my kit – I took my own French clothes, but agents checked them over to make sure nothing English crept in.

The SOE forgers supplied my papers – a fifteen-year-old girl named Marie Yvette Laplage, a distant relation of Madame Bernadotte Ferrier who lived on a farm just outside Bruneval. The forgers gave me a letter from her, inviting me to live with her. My parents were dead and she was my sole surviving relative. A story all too common given the war, I supposed.

I checked my radio and its spares a final time. It came alive when turned on and I heard morse chatter when I swung across the frequencies. We were due to take off at zero-one-hundred, flying for about an hour to the landing site south of Étretat. I lay down once everything had been checked and tried to sleep, expecting to lie there reviewing details of the operation ... until a WAAF woke me with a ubiquitous mug of tea.

"I was sent to wake you up, Miss. It's twenty-three-thirty."

I rubbed my eyes. "Thank you." I sat up, sipping my tea, clearing the sleep from my head. Falling asleep was a surprise: tension ran through me but excitement was holding fear at bay.

Tea finished, I left the tiny room, to find Maurice Buckmaster waiting for me.

"There's been a change of plans, Marie."

My heart sank – he'd cancelled the operation.

"It's been decided that leaving you in France risks the operation, the Resistance will watch and let us know if things change. You'll be brought home once you've got us the information we need. We'll send instructions for your pick-up by radio and you're to leave the radio with Colonel Rémy."

Not cancelled ...

I let out a soft breath, strangely relieved. "Yes, sir."

"Good luck, Marie."

"Thank you, sir."

I sat in the right-hand seat in the Lysander with a Sten in my lap to "fend off any unwanted attention on landing" according to my laconic pilot. I had a great but scary view out of the cockpit: once we crossed the English coast; we descended until our wheels seemed to skate along the waves but the pilot laughed, assuring me we were at least fifty feet above them. Approaching the coast, we climbed and my pilot shared a thumbs up when he identified our landfall at La Falaise d'Amont in broken moonlight. A few minutes later we saw a light flash in Morse and the pilot flicked a downward pointing light in our reply. Three lights appeared and the engine noise fell away as we descended rapidly towards them. I saw some trees flick below us in the landing lights and then we bumped and bounced to a stop. I unlatched my window and hefted the Sten onto the ledge. The pilot spun the plane round and ran back down the field before turning again, ready to leave.

Figures ran across the field from the hedge but no helmeted soldiers. One came to the foot of the ladder. "Marie?"

"Colonel Rémy?"

"D'accord."

I handed the Sten to the pilot. We had additional luggage beside my case and radio. I passed it all down and smiled at the pilot. "Thanks for the ride."

He smiled and waved me down the steps, reaching across to lock the door once I was down. The engine picked up and with a couple of flicks of the rudder the Lysander roared down the field and into the air.

France.

My heart sang – with all its dangers, I'd come home, taking the fight to the *Boche*.

One of the men grabbed my arm, pointing at the bags we had unloaded. "Which ones are yours?"

"Those two." I pointed at my bags.

Colonel Rémy directed his men to take the rest of the luggage then turned to me.

"Welcome to France."

"Thank you, but it's back to France. I am from ..."

"No." He interrupted me. "No. Never tell anyone about before the war. The *Boche* will use your family and friends against you." His eyes bored into mine in the dim moonlight.

I gulped – the joy of being back in France had me forgetting the importance of security.

Colonel Rémy picked up the radio case and indicated for me to take my bag. "Follow me."

We went through a gap in the hedge onto a farm track and walked several kilometres to a cottage on the edge of a ploughed field. The cold and musty interior offered a bleak welcome.

Colonel Rémy found a candle in a drawer and checked the shutters were closed. The candle revealed a tiny kitchen in its flickering light. "No-one lives here now. The *Boche* swept up the farm worker that lived here in the forced labour draft." His eyes travelled round the cottage and the light of the candle revealed his drawn face, the lines accentuated by the shadows. "There are many empty cottages like this."

France under the Nazis was a foreign country.

I inspected the cold kitchen range.

Colonel Rémy shook his head. "You cannot light the stove, Marie – the smoke will give you away."

I sighed but understood the danger.

"You will stay here tonight and tomorrow morning, then we'll move you closer to Bruneval. Stay inside until then."

With that, he left and I watched his figure fade into the darkness down the track. I picked up the candle and explored: a bedroom containing a bed and a heap of musty-smelling blankets.

***

When I woke, my breath steamed in the freezing air. I lay under the weight of the heaped blankets, unwilling to leave their meagre warmth. But nature called and I visited the privy across the yard. The clatter of the hand-pump shocked the still air and I froze, straining for any answering sound.

Reassured by the silence after half a minute, I pumped the well and a stream of icy water allowed me to wash my face and hands.

In the light of day, I inspected the cottage; the kitchen contained no food, just some dirty cooking utensils. The cupboard in the bedroom contained a pair of old boots shedding their soles and flakes of dried mud. Whoever had lived here had taken what meagre belongings they possessed when shipped out. I took a battered saucepan out to the pump, washed and filled it with fresh water for the day.

Colonel Rémy told me not to leave the cottage, but Airsaig had drummed into us the importance of always having an escape route. I spent an hour or so surveying the surrounding country while keeping out of sight. The track stopped at the cottage. A ploughed field occupied two of its sides providing no cover for over a hundred metres to a hedgerow. On the other two sides lay a fallow field, with tussocky grass and thistles that promised some cover – and a hedge about thirty metres away. Crouching low, I moved across the field to the hedge. After watching and listening, I clambered through a gap to find a shallow ditch on the far side, running towards a patch of woods. I had my escape route if danger came up the track.

Back in the cottage, I pictured the radio operators at Bletchley sitting where I had sat, waiting for incoming messages, switching between frequencies according to the agents' schedules. I did not need to transmit tonight but I could be instructed to listen for a message: after the BBC news, a dozen or so phrases were broadcast that told people like me to listen out at my designated times or for a *Maquis* group to blow up a particular bridge; but most phrases were complete rubbish to confuse the *Boche*.

As the pale sun dragged itself across the sky behind thin sheets of cloud, I rehearsed my code poem in my head and listened out for any sign of people approaching the cottage, pistol close to hand.

Late in the morning a distant rattle alerted me and I hid behind the low wood pile with the fallow field behind me, pistol at the ready. A tall man on a bicycle appeared. He dismounted, propped the bicycle against a fence post and walked towards the cottage, calling out softly in French.

"Marie, Marie. I'm Marcel. Colonel Rémy sent me."

I stayed in my hiding place, covering him with my pistol. "How do you know Marie?"

"You arrived here early this morning," his face split into an engaging smile. "And I expect you'd like lunch." He hefted the bag hanging from his shoulder.

I walked round the end of the wood pile, still covering him with my pistol.

"Put the bag on the ground and step back."

Marcel arched an eyebrow but lowered the bag and took a couple of steps back, watching my pistol.

"*Reculez.*" I waved him back, my pistol steady on his body.

He moved further back.

Keeping my eye and pistol on him. I flipped the cover off the leather bag to reveal a loaf of bread, a bottle of wine and what from the aroma promised to be cheese and a crock of some preserved meat.

"Thank you. I am quite hungry." I closed the bag and picked it up, giving Marcel a smile. "Care to join me for lunch?" I waved towards the cottage.

He glanced at my pistol. "Perhaps, mademoiselle, you might stop waving the pistol in my direction?"

I blushed, clicked on the safety and put the pistol in my pocket.

Over a lunch of wine, cheese, crusty bread and *rillette de lapin*, Marcel relayed the plans for the rest of the day as my taste buds revelled in the meal, the best I'd had since leaving France. The RAF served mush in comparison.

Marcel waved the wine bottle airily. "After lunch, we will walk to the road where a truck will pick you up and take you to a safe house outside Bruneval. Colonel Rémy will meet you there."

I nodded, my mouth full of bread and cheese.

We finished eating and gathered up our stuff. Marcel balanced the radio case on his bicycle handlebars, walking beside me with my other case pulling at my arm. We reached the road and hid ourselves in the hedge while we waited. After about fifteen minutes we heard a vehicle approaching.

Marcel cocked his ear. "*Boche.* Stay down."

A minute later, a *Wehrmacht* truck rolled past, half-a-dozen soldiers sitting in the back, eyes searching out across the countryside, rifles standing between their knees. As they disappeared round the bend, I started to rise but Marcel pressed me back down. A moment later, a *Wehrmacht* scout car went past with an officer seated in the back. We watched it roll down the road and round the corner.

Marcel's hand left my back and he leaned across, mouth beside my ear. "There's frequently an officer vehicle following patrols like that."

I nodded.

Something to remember...

Minutes later we heard a different sounding vehicle. It didn't thrum like the well-maintained *Wehrmacht* vehicles and an arhythmic set of rattles supplemented its wheezing engine – a farm truck.

I smiled at Marcel, nodding in understanding as he extricated himself from the hedge. The truck, its tray loaded with some sort of root vegetable, stopped. Marcel shared a nod with the truck driver who leapt from the cab, moving the vegetables away and dropping the side of a hidden compartment to reveal a low volume concealed beneath the heaped vegetables.

Marcel shoved the radio case in and grabbed my bag, shoving it in as well. "Get in."

I gave him an uncomprehending look and he picked me up round my knees and shoulders, pushing me into the narrow gap.

I gasped as the side of the box slammed back up, leaving me in dingy gloom. I heard vegetables being heaped back to cover my hiding place.

I heard Marcel' voice. "Stay quiet – whatever happens, stay quiet. We need to get you past the guard post on the road into Bruneval. The coast is a restricted area."

The truck got underway and as it lurched along the road, I tried to find a comfortable position where my head wasn't bouncing between the deck below and the boards above. About half an hour later, the truck rolled to a stop and I heard German voices.

My stomach tightened as the truck leaned – one of the soldiers climbing onto the side of the tray. With my head resting on my arms, I heard the thumping of my heart as the truck shifted beneath the German soldier as he moved around. After a minute, the truck lurched and boots crunched on the road as he jumped off. A shout in German and the truck started moving again.

We drove on, swaying through the twisty country lanes. Then the truck slowed, turned and came to a stop. They shifted the vegetables and the compartment opened. Marcel stood there smiling at me in the gloom of a barn. "Out you come, Marie."

I clambered to the ground, then reached back in to retrieve my cases.

"Follow me."

Marcel grabbed my cases and led me though a side door of the barn, across a narrow yard and into a farmhouse. I found myself in a warm kitchen redolent with the heady smell of baking bread. Marcel set down the cases and left, with a nod to the two men sitting at a large table, one of them Colonel Rémy, hair greying around his temples.

"Welcome again, Marie." Colonel Rémy stood and leaned across to shake my hand. "This is Guillaume who will be working with you." He gestured at a chair. "Please take a seat and we will discuss our plans."

I nodded at Guillaume as I sat, then looked across at Colonel Rémy. "London needs the size of German forces here in Bruneval and the surrounding area."

Guillaume frowned, leaning towards me. "Why?"

I opened my mouth, but Colonel Remy placed a hand on Guillaume's arm. "That's not for us to know – and, anyway, I doubt Marie knows." He glanced across at me before turning back to Guillaume. "We assemble the information London needs and Marie sends it."

I waited for him to continue – and then spoke into his silence. "London's interest in Bruneval must remain secret." I gathered their nods of agreement before continuing. "Now, what about the German forces in Bruneval?"

Colonel Rémy sat back. "They have three bunkers guarding the beach with half a dozen soldiers in each one all the time – a machine gun crew – with an officer or senior NCO in the command bunker. That's fitted with a multi-barrel flak gun as well. It's the one closest to the road, furthest from the beach. During the day they sometimes exercise on the beach. There's fifty of them, but they're not frontline troops;" His voice held condescension and disbelief. "It's taken about half an hour on occasion for them to stand-to in the bunkers from their barracks above the village."

Half an hour?

My eyebrows rose in surprise. "We need to find out their unit – and an exact number if possible."

Colonel Remy nodded. "Then there's something happening on the clifftop."

The RDF station.

I bottled up my reaction. "Hmm?"

"We're not sure what it's for as we can't get close to it." He scowled. "But that tells us it's important to the *Boche.*"

Guillaume leaned forward. "It's important enough for them to put up another barracks close by."

I nodded. "We need to find out the troop numbers up there – and their unit."

Colonel Rémy nodded. "We think they number between one and two hundred troops."

London would not like that but we needed a better idea of their numbers. "What about reinforcements?"

Colonel Rémy thought for a moment. "There's half a regiment at Goderville; that's about 1,500 troops with some trucks and light armoured vehicles. Goderville is about four hours march away." He shrugged. "Longer again at night, but their few motorised units might arrive here in about an hour ... perhaps a hundred and fifty troops and a couple of armoured cars."

I sat back, thinking about my briefing. "How do we find out the number of troops in the barracks and their unit?"

Colonel Rémy's eyes held mine. "We will find a way."

"And the regiment in Goderville?"

Colonel Rémy smiled. "I can get that information tomorrow or the day after, perhaps by then also the name of the commander. The *Boche* sent most of their combat troops to the eastern front, fighting the Russians, their best commanders too." He pursed his lips. "But they still have some quality troops here in France with competent and battle-hardened commanders."

I nodded. "Do I need to go into Bruneval myself?"

Colonel Rémy shook his head. "Definitely not. That's too dangerous – the *Boche* thoroughly check everyone in and out of the village. Members of the *Maquis* there give us detailed information when things change."

"Okay." It would be stupid to needlessly stick my head into a hornet's nest.

"Now, let us show you to your room and get your radio hidden." He frowned. "You understand that you must not transmit from here?" His eyes held mine until I nodded. "When you need to send information, we will find a place for you – never the same place. The *Boche* listen out all over France to triangulate illegal transmissions. They have interception vans on constant patrol."

My training had covered this. "Of course."

Guillaume took me upstairs to a tiny room where the bed took up most of the space. It had a large carved headboard that looked to be part of the wall. "Watch. You must close the door." He swung it shut and reached his hand up under the bed. I heard a faint click and the headboard sagged forward. He pushed the pillows out of the way and the board dropped down to reveal a space easily large enough for the radio case.

"You try. Feel for a section you must press."

I closed the hidden compartment and then reached under the bed searching with my fingers for the release. I had to feel around for it but after a couple of false starts I found a section that depressed and the headboard fell away. I placed the radio case inside the cavity, pushing the headboard up until it clicked back into place.

Guillaume opened the bedroom door. "Try it now."

I knew where to press but with the door open, nothing happened and we shared a smile of understanding.

"Please join us for supper in the kitchen." Guillaume gestured to the stairs.

Colonel Rémy had left and a middle-aged woman stood at the kitchen range. She turned as we entered, her face blank. "Sit down."

"Yes, mother," Guillaume responded, indicating a chair for me.

We ate a thick vegetable soup and fresh bread – delicious – but sat in complete silence. Guillaume's mother tried her best to ignore me, perhaps scared of her son's involvement in the resistance and the danger I brought into her house.

***

In the morning, Guillaume took me walking across the farm, herding a small flock of sheep up onto a higher field. From there, I had an uninterrupted view towards the coast. About two miles away I saw the house on the cliff associated with the German radar station. About a quarter of a mile from that squatted some long, low buildings surrounded by a tall fence – the barracks. I turned my back to them and let my gaze roam over the farm and its buildings. If the *Boche* were watching, I did not want to seem too interested in the barracks.

"We'll leave the sheep here as this gives someone a reason to come out and spend time here." Guillaume said. "I've a dependable boy who will come up here to watch the sheep every day and tell me about anything interesting over there." He nodded his head towards the barracks.

They involved children in the Maquis?

"Is everyone in the resistance?"

Guillaume shook his head, frowning at my stupidity. "No, of course not." He stood, staring at the sheep as they cropped the grass, oblivious to the dark human danger around them. "For the couple of boys working with me, they know me and no-one else." He turned, his face serious. "I know only Colonel Rémy and Marcel." His eyes swept across the village. "I don't need to know anyone else, so I don't." I heard the tension in his voice, saw it in his body.

Living with this fear of exposure day in, day out, year after year must be exhausting.

We walked back to the farmhouse, finding Colonel Rémy there. "We will deliver vegetables to the barracks tomorrow." His eyes lingered on me. "You could view the site in person before you return to England."

I felt my stomach tighten. Colonel Remy watched.

This was a test. A test of me, perhaps? Of London? If I didn't go, would they stop helping?

My skin prickled with the realisation: I had to go.

"Okay." I held my breathing steady, but felt my heartbeat accelerate.

A hint of a smile touched his lips. "You could pass for a farmer's daughter in the right clothes." His eyes swept me again. "I'll get some to you later today"

"And the information about the unit in Goderville?"

Colonel Rémy shook his head. "Not yet – tomorrow, I think."

"If all goes well tomorrow then, I'll need to transmit tomorrow night."

"We don't want to transmit anywhere near Bruneval and that means getting you and your radio out of the coastal zone." Colonel Rémy's face became thoughtful. "Once the information is transmitted, will you need to return here?"

"I don't think so," I thought for a moment. "I'm supposed to be picked up after they get the information."

Colonel Remy pursed his lips. "Let's hope they're happy with what we send them. Crossing the coastal checkpoints is always a risk."

He beckoned to Guillaume. "Come with me, please." He nodded. "Until tomorrow, Marie."

Later that day Guillaume returned with a package of clothes. They fitted well enough for wartime – coarse working clothes for a farm girl.

***

In the morning, I helped Guillaume load potatoes, turnips and onions in wooden boxes onto the back of a bedraggled farm truck. I just managed to lift some of the heavy boxes and became quite grubby in the process.

Before we climbed into the cab, Guillaume grabbed my shoulder. "Don't speak to anyone. Just stay silent."

I nodded – and the butterflies commenced quivering their wings in anticipation.

Guillaume started the truck. It wheezed out of the yard towards the village, but we soon turned off onto a gravelled track. I thought about the photomosaic of the area I had studied at Tempsford.

Ah yes – the single track to the barracks from inland.

At one point we splashed through a shallow stream gurgling down the valley. After a kilometre or so, a roadblock appeared ahead – with two guards.

Guillaume wound down his window.

One of the guards walked round the barricade. "Papers?"

Guillaume produced a letter with the Swastika at the top – the order for the vegetables, I presumed.

The guard handed it back, glancing at the boxes of vegetables on the truck. "Identity cards."

I handed my forged card to Guillaume who passed it on to the guard. The butterflies accelerated – but the guard barely glanced at it.

He passed it back and waved at his colleague. "Let them through."

As Guillaume put the truck into gear, I saw the guard on the field telephone, telling the barracks of our approach. We wound our way round the shoulder of a gentle hill, arriving at another guard post at the gate into the compound. There was a track leading off across the hill – towards the RDF station. We produced our papers again and the guard directed us towards one of the buildings.

A Wehrmacht soldier wearing an apron directed us alongside a loading dock and then clambered onto the truck. I sat, unsure what to do.

Guillaume frowned at me. "Get out. We must help unload it."

The cook finished inspecting the vegetables and jerked his head towards the cookhouse. He then stood back, crossing his arms – unloading was our responsibility.

Guillaume handed the order to the cook, pointing out the place for his signature. Then he picked up a box and I followed his lead. The cook led us inside into the mess hall and pointed at a storeroom. We deposited our boxes and then returned for another one as the cook counted them off.

By the time the truck was half unloaded, sweat ran down my body under my clothes and my arms ached. After depositing my latest box, I stopped and leant against the messroom wall, breathing deeply and shaking my arms to relieve the strain. I needed an excuse to survey the mess hall and this seemed my best opportunity.

The cook stared at me, then shook his head at my lack of stamina before heading back outside. I sat on one of the benches beside the tables, gauging the number of people who could sit each side.

As Guillaume carried in another load, the cook came back and marched up to where I sat, waving his arms and yelling at me.

Aggression and superiority inflated him as he towered above me and he grabbed my arm, pulling me to my feet. I had no idea what he had said but understood what he wanted. I dragged out to help Guillaume finish unloading the boxes and stacking them in the storeroom. The cook then pointed to a stack of empty boxes on the dock which we loaded onto the truck as the cook watched. By the time we finished, sweat soaked parts of my grubby clothing, despite the winter chill. I clambered into the truck's cabin with arms like string. But walking to and fro unloading the truck I'd seen between the buildings: another gate allowed entry at the far end of the compound, closed but unguarded, though a couple of guards ambled on patrol outside the wire.

Guillaume walked up to the cook – his hand out for the order. The cook grunted and took a pen from his jacket pocket, scrawling a signature on the paper before handing it back to Guillaume, who nodded in acknowledgement.

We returned through the checkpoints without problem arriving back at the farmyard about three hours after we'd left. By then, my sweat-dampened clothes scratched and itched against my skin.

Colonel Rémy sat in the farmhouse kitchen, waiting for us. "Well?"

Guillaume pointed his chin at me. "Ask her."

I thought about what I'd seen before replying. "There are eight tables in the mess hall, with benches either side. From sitting on one of them, each bench will fit six *Boche* arses. That's ninety-six soldiers at a sitting." I pursed my lips. "They must have two sittings, given the number of barrack blocks ... and they have a large food store for just a hundred soldiers." I glanced across at Guillaume, who nodded in agreement. I told Colonel Rémy about the track off to the installation on the cliffs, the checkpoint, guard house, fence, second gate and guards ambling round the outside of the enclosure.

Colonel Rémy nodded. "That aligns with what I know." He gazed past me for a moment. "The information from Goderville is that the hilltop barrack troops come from that half regiment – about one hundred and fifty men with their officers. They rotate every month or so and the amount of transport used fits that number. The troops are from the Baltic states that the Nazis conscripted into military service – but with mostly *Boche* NCOs and officers. That means they're garrison troops and not a front-line unit. The commander in Goderville is a fat *Boche*, more interested in his food than his troops."

"Thank you." I sent him a quick smile. "I need to send this information to London as soon as possible."

"That's set up for tonight. We just need to get you out of the coastal zone."

"Is there time for me to wash and change my clothes?"

Colonel Rémy nodded and I headed up to my room. I stripped and washed myself using a jug of cold water, bowl and rags, shivering and thinking of Claire's elegant flat in London and its well-appointed bathroom. Somewhere back in England was a hot bath with my name on it.

Once dressed in my own clothes, I gathered up my things. Out in the farmyard, I managed the climb into the hidden compartment myself after hoisting in my case and the one with the radio. Then they stacked empty boxes above me. We made it past the coastal zone checkpoint with no problems and I again rested my head on my arms as the truck jounced along on its tired springs.

"Pull over, it's a *Boche* patrol." Colonel Rémy's loud voice instructed Guillaume – and warned me of the danger.

We moved to the side of the road and waited with the engine off. Through a crack I saw a Wehrmacht truck rumble past and then I heard it stop and boots approached, crunching in the gravel: polished boots – an officer.

"Papers, identity cards." The officer spoke reasonable French.

I realised that I'd put my pistol in my case – and I couldn't get at it. *Imbecile.*

"Where are you going – and why?"

I felt the truck move as a soldier clambered up to inspect the boxes.

"We have to get another load vegetables for the barracks at Bruneval."

I heard some papers rustle and Colonel Rémy's voice joined in. "This is the letter authorising our travel from the commandant at Goderville."

I heard the soldier moving around above me as I lay hardly daring to breathe.

The officer's voice rang out to his soldier on the truck. The man replied and I felt the truck rock as he jumped off.

"Go, fetch our vegetables then."

I heard the *ennui* in the lieutenant's voice, followed by an engine starting.

The silence grew before Colonel Rémy spoke. "Let's go."

The engine shuddered into life and I breathed again. We drove on for about another thirty minutes before the truck stopped and I once again smelled a farmyard. Doors scraped open and the truck lurched forward into dimness.

Colonel Rémy dropped the side and I clambered out.

"You'll stay here until later tonight. Then we'll take you to where you can transmit."

"I'll need some paper to prepare my message."

"Of course."

We went from the barn to the farmhouse, leaving my radio and case in the truck. I sat in the kitchen preparing my message, trying to pack all the information into the smallest number of words to keep the transmission time as low as possible. It was an interesting exercise in brevity without sacrificing clarity. Once I had it in English, I encoded it using my poem, tore up the working copies, dropped them into the kitchen range and watched them burn, stirring with the poker to break the burnt paper into fragments. I put the coded message in my sock and retied my shoe.

I'd got it down to just over eighty, five-character code groups, taking about four minutes to send at a careful twenty words a minute. That was enough for the SD (the *Sicherheitsdienst* – the intelligence service of the SS) listening posts and vans to get a fix. Allowing for receiving a return message, I estimated it all at about six minutes after I started transmitting. Wherever we transmitted from, we had to get away without delay – and without attracting attention.

Colonel Rémy returned after dark and I explained what I needed.

He nodded. "I have such a place. We will leave here in about an hour and walk there – about half an hour. After you're finished, we'll take you back to that cottage."

We walked through a light drizzle for half-an-hour, then Colonel Rémy led me into a shack hiding in a copse. "This is it, Marie." He lifted the radio case onto a wooden shelf.

"Thank you." I checked my watch: fifteen minutes to my transmission time at ten to the hour. I pulled a rag out of my pocket and wiped the rain from the radio case – water in the radio might wreck it. With that done, I lifted the lid, connected the aerial, morse key and headset. I removed my shoe and sock to retrieve the coded message. I smoothed out the paper and weighted it with my watch. I read through the code groups using a shaded torch.

"I'll need you to hold the torch on the paper while I transmit."

Colonel Rémy nodded.

I put a pencil beside the message and kept my eye on the time, turning on the set with five minutes to go. Once the set warmed up, I scanned round the dial catching snatches of morse: the set worked fine. I tuned to my frequency and pictured someone sitting where I had sat for a year at Bletchley. They were now waiting for a transmission from me.

"Torch, please."

Colonel Rémy shaded the light from the torch onto the message. I re-positioned the headset and sent my recognition code, flicking back to receive. The correct response came back in dots and dashes. I switched to send and started transmitting, the training about accuracy not speed playing in my head as the message flowed out through my hand.

I ended with my recognition code, switched to receive, flipped over the message paper and picked up the pencil, waiting for a reply.

The radio repeated my recognition code into the headphones and that was followed by a short stream of morse that I copied down. The message ended and I sent my code in acknowledgement. Working swiftly, I switched off the set, stowing the aerial, pencil, headset and key then closed the case. Refolding the message paper, I again stowed it in my sock, put on my shoe and laced it up.

I grabbed my watch. "Let's go."

Colonel Rémy took the radio case, leaving my lighter one to me and we walked through the wood, to a waiting car. Colonel Rémy directed me into the back with my two cases and we accelerated away. For about twenty minutes, we drove along farm tracks. I grabbed the radio case, holding it on my lap in an effort to shield it from the worst of the bounces and jerks.

Colonel Rémy signalled the car to stop. "We walk again from here."

We tried to dodge the puddles as we walked through the persistent drizzle until I recognised the cottage where I had spent the first night. With the shutters closed and a candle lit, I retrieved the message paper from my sock and decoded it.

RETURN B29 12140230

They were going to pick me up at 0230 hours on 14 December – in just over a day – but I had no idea about B29 and turned to Colonel Rémy.

He smiled. "You'll leave by air from somewhere not too far from here."

I listened to the rain dripping from the eaves. "Let's hope the weather clears by then."

He nodded and then explored the cupboards. "Ah – supper."

I wished from inside my damp clothes that we could use the stove – but we could not risk the smoke. The SD would have sent out patrols to try and find us. We sat at the table and started on our cold meal.

"You're staying with me until I leave?"

"Yes. We will meet up with the reception party tomorrow evening," he smiled, grimly. "They don't know you."

I understood: I had to be vouched for by him.

"Now, we should get some sleep." He waved me towards the single bedroom. "I'll sleep on that bench."

We made ourselves as comfortable as the primitive setting allowed and I drifted off to sleep under my share of the musty blankets, feeling great satisfaction: I had accomplished my mission.

December 1941 – May 1942

In the morning the sky cleared, with rags of cloud from the previous day's rain fleeing before a breeze. We made use of the privy and the pump in the yard, spending the morning in silence. About midday I heard the rattle of what I suspected was a bicycle. Both of us grabbed our pistols and Colonel Rémy slipped out of the door. I waited by the bedroom window, watching through a crack in the shutters.

Marcel clambered off his bicycle with a large bag. As before, he brought a meal.

Colonel Rémy walked out to him. "Tell Jacques to meet us at the farm outside Fongueusemare by nine o'clock, with the landing lights."

Marcel nodded, mounted the bicycle and waved. "*Au revoir.*"

The rest of the day passed in deep silence, each of us with our own thoughts. Idle talk could reveal personal details of other people that might assist the *Boche* if interrogated. As dusk fell, Colonel Rémy roused me and we ate the remaining food.

"We'll leave here in an hour. There's a half-hour walk and then we'll meet my crew and head to the landing site."

At the appointed time we set off across the fields carrying my cases and met Colonel Rémy's crew waiting in a car. The combination of farm tracks at night without any lights and this driver was a wild experience I don't want to repeat. On one occasion we skidded along the edge of a ditch for several metres.

Once we arrived, Colonel Rémy walked the field to find the driest line and directed his crew to set up the lights in the usual L-shaped pattern, without turning them on.

"Shall I leave the radio case on the back seat?" I asked Colonel Rémy.

He nodded.

We waited in the hedgerow until we heard the faint sound of an aeroengine. The sound grew and Colonel Rémy flashed his torch in the recognition signal. The plane flashed back. Colonel Rémy turned on the landing light at this end and then directed his torch down the landing line, flashing his crew there to turn on their lights.

From there things went as planned: once landed, the Lysander taxied back to where we waited and we offloaded several inbound cases. I hoisted my case up and clambered in after them. The pilot opened the throttle as I settled into my seat. We bounced down the field as I struggled with my straps, just getting them fastened as we lifted over the trees.

I found and fitted my headset. "Good morning, thanks for the lift."

I saw the pilot's quick smile lit by the dim red glow from the instruments before he returned to scanning ahead, where the treetops flew past just below the nose.

My headset crackled. "Good morning to you, ma'am. I think I saw a night fighter above me when I crossed the coast, so we'll stay low and lost in the weeds."

I nodded: they had no chance of picking us up in the clutter of ground returns. "What about the coastal flak?"

"That's not a problem. We'll slip out through a gap," In the dim, red light, I watched his finger following a track line on his map.

Minutes later I caught a glimpse of the channel ahead of us and we sped across some dunes with a finger of tracer groping for us across the sky.

I heard the smile in the pilot's voice. "They're awake."

"I thought we were going through a gap?"

The pilot risked a quick glance in my direction. "There are bunkers dotted all up and down the coast. Sometimes they're sufficiently awake to fire wildly in my direction – but all they hit is empty sky."

The rest of the trip passed in silence and we landed safely at Tempsford.

We taxied in and the propeller jerked to a stop, the engine ticking as it cooled. I lifted off my headset and smiled at the pilot. "Thanks for the ride."

"A pleasure ma'am."

I chuckled, noticing the flight lieutenant bars on his shoulders. "I'm not a ma'am, sir – I'm just a corporal."

The pilot turned from his door, admiration on his face. "Ma'am, what you've been doing in France makes you "ma'am" in my book." He held my gaze for a second and then climbed down.

I found an LAC waiting for me. "Hand down the bags, ma'am."

I let that go and lifted my case from behind me, passing it to the LAC.

He picked it up. "Follow me. Please ma'am."

He led me to a staff car with blacked out windows waiting on the concrete, depositing my cases in the boot. As we approached, the rear door swung open towards me and I climbed in – to find Maurice Buckmaster sitting there.

"Welcome back, Miss Roberts," he said with a nod of acknowledgement. "We're heading back to London so relax. We'll debrief back at HQ later today." He passed me a thermos and a pack of sandwiches wrapped in greaseproof paper. "Breakfast."

Does he meet all returning agents?

The hot, sweet tea was welcome, if a trifle awkward in the back of a moving vehicle and I ate one of the ubiquitous meat-paste sandwiches. All the while Mr Buckmaster read through papers in the dim lamp light, pulling folder after folder from his case, occasionally scribbling a note. As I wedged myself into the corner trying to sleep, he glanced at me and then returned to his work.

Does he ever sleep?

I woke as we negotiated the streets into London, pulling up in front of a building I recognised in Montagu Square.

Mr Buckmaster leaned across with a smile. "Here's the keys. Your usual room awaits. Report back to HQ by twelve hundred hours."

"Yes, sir." I stifled a yawn.

I climbed out and the driver handed me my case. "Thank you."

I watched him climb back in and the car depart, then turned wearily, climbed the steps and turned the key in the front door. When I arrived at flat 2, Claire greeted me, dressed for work.

"Welcome back. The same room's ready and I expect you'd like a bath?"

"Yes, please."

She nodded. "There's a bag in your room with all your stuff. I'll see you at HQ later today."

I smiled my thanks and headed to the bedroom. Thirty minutes later I set my alarm for eleven and dropped into bed.

***

I found my ID card and pass in my bag when the alarm woke me. I had no uniform so I dressed in civvies but my ID card and pass made my arrival at

HQ simple. I needed no escort through to section F where they told me Mr Buckmaster wanted to speak to me shortly, so I took a seat.

He appeared, a briefcase swinging from one hand. "Come with me please Miss Roberts. We're off to a meeting in the War Office."

I jumped to my feet. "Sir."

He led me to the back of the building and a waiting car. Once seated, he turned to me. "There will be senior officers at this meeting and I don't want you browbeaten by anyone." He frowned. "You're the person with recent experience of Bruneval. If people ask you things that you don't know, say so. If you state an opinion, explain your reasons for it."

I swallowed. "Yes, sir."

The guard outside the offices inspected our passes and waved us through the sandbagged entrance into an imposing building of Portland stone. As we entered, a naval lieutenant turned from chatting with the female receptionist, also in naval uniform.

"Mr Buckmaster?"

"Yes – and my assistant."

"Come with me."

We followed him up the polished stairs of this Victorian edifice, where only the cross-hatched tape on the windows nodded towards the war. He gestured us into a conference room where half a dozen officers from the three services sat. I smothered a gasp – there were a Group Captain, a Rear Admiral and a Brigadier General at the table – a daunting collection of brass – along with a sprinkling of more junior officers. My stomach lurched and I tried to swallow the inevitable butterflies.

The Rear Admiral remained seated as we entered. "Ah, Mr Buckmaster, I presume."

"Sir."

"Well, sit down, sit down – and please introduce us to your assistant."

Mr Buckmaster remained standing. "I'm sorry, sir, but I understood that my assistant would remain anonymous, for security reasons."

The senior officers leaned back in their chairs, spreading a distinctly frosty silence, unused to refusal.

The Rear Admiral frowned and Mr Buckmaster returned his gaze without wavering. A long second of silence passed before the Rear Admiral dropped

his eyes and nodded. "Very well." He turned to me. "Welcome, er … Miss."
He nodded at a naval lieutenant who removed a cloth covering from the wall,
revealing the photomosaic I had seen at RAF Tempsford.

"Miss … er … Miss, please walk us through the troop dispositions around
Bruneval."

I glanced at Mr Buckmaster who sent me on my way with an encouraging
nod. I walked round the table to the photomosaic, trying to summon some
saliva into my dry mouth. I stared at the map, bringing my thoughts into an
organised stream.

"The troops in the area are garrison troops – conscripts from the Baltic
states overrun by the Nazis." I stopped and half turned to my audience – I'd
been speaking to the map. I swallowed the sudden excess of saliva. "They have
some regular Wehrmacht NCOs and the officers are Wehrmacht. They man the
shore defences at Bruneval all the time – at least six troops armed with machine
guns in each of the three bunkers, including the command bunker, which has
a flak cannon as well as a machine gun." I tapped each of the bunkers on the
photomosaic with a trembling finger. "They can take up to thirty minutes to
muster." I saw the Brigadier General sniff at that news. "Their barracks are here,"
I stiffened my hand to suppress the trembling before I tapped the map. "And
this is the path from their barracks down to the village." I turned from the
mosaic. "The *Maquis* provided this information. I did not go into the village
myself."

The Brigadier General erupted. "Why not? Second-hand information is
dubious, at best."

I blanched at this and glanced at Mr Buckmaster, who indicated I should
answer. "Sir, the *Maquis* in the town watch the soldiers all the time and report
if things change. Entering the village risked unnecessary discovery."

The Brigadier General snorted in derision, his face making it clear what he
thought of someone unwilling to take a risk to verify important information. I
felt myself blush at the implication.

Mr Buckmaster leaned forward, his tone severe. "Brigadier, my agent's
character is not in question. She correctly assessed the situation. Her capture
risked alerting the enemy to our interest in the town, something we need to
avoid at all costs."

The Brigadier harumphed.

Mr Buckmaster nodded to me. "Continue, please."

I pointed to the barrack buildings near the radar station on the cliffs. "These buildings house no more than one hundred and fifty troops, NCOs and their officers. As with the troops in the town, they are part of the half-regiment stationed at Goderville and rotate through this location about every month."

The Brigadier's voice dripped sarcasm. "I suppose the French resistance provided those figures as well?" He glanced round the table, shaking his head.

His attitude was getting to me, but I fought down a sharp response. "No sir. I visited the site myself, delivering vegetables to the cook house with a member of the *Maquis*. I counted eight tables in the mess hall, with benches for six Germans each side."

I caught Mr Buckmaster's frown.

Had I let my irritation show?

"The mess hall seats ninety-six people. Based on the observations of the *Maquis* and my personal inspection of the large storerooms in the cookhouse, we surmise they have two sittings for each meal. The Maquis also calculate one hundred and fifty officers and men based on the amount of motor transport used when relieved from Goderville. This, together with the number of barrack blocks, tallies with my observations."

The Brigadier harumphed again and I noticed Mr Buckmaster stir in his seat.

I pointed to the photomosaic again, picking out the track we had used with a finger that no longer trembled. "A single road – a farm track – leads to the barracks from the inland side. It fords a stream here." I tapped the map again. "There is a guard post and gate about here." Another tap. "It had two privates manning it when we went through and connects by field telephone to the barracks. There's a guard house here," I tapped the mosaic. "And another gate here on the other side of the compound opposite the guard house. The compound has a seven-foot-high barbed wire fence. I saw two soldiers patrolling outside the fence. Another track from the guard house leads onto the cliffs."

A major leant forward. "What can you tell us about that half regiment at ..." He checked his notes. "At Goderville?"

"It's full of conscripts from the Baltic states, poorly trained and not well led." I risked a smile. "Their commander loves his food and shows little interest in his troops." I noticed this major had paratrooper wings on his uniform. "There are about fifteen hundred officers and men at Goderville, with a few light armoured vehicles and trucks – enough to move about one hundred and fifty troops at a time. Allowing for mustering, Goderville is about an hour away from Bruneval in a truck. The remainder must march the ten miles once they have assembled – about four hours, again allowing for mustering."

The major jotted in his notebook. "Thank you, Miss."

Mr Buckmaster raised an eyebrow at me. "Anything else?"

I glanced back at the mosaic and shook my head.

"Questions, gentlemen?"

Heads shook and people started to rise. Then the major interrupted the general exit. "Yes, sir – I have a question."

Everyone settled back into their seats.

"What can you tell me about the countryside around Bruneval, Miss?"

I turned to him as realisation swept through me.

He was to command an airborne attack to capture the Boche radar system.

Our eyes met in unspoken understanding and then I turned back to the mosaic. "It's rolling farmland with open fields and the occasional copse or wood inland from the coast." I drew my fingers along the shore. "The strip along the clifftops is fenced off and uncultivated, with patches of brambles and undergrowth growing wild." My hand moved inland, following a hedgerow. "Most fields are bounded by hedges and some of those are dense, perhaps strengthened with wire: they keep sheep." I smiled at the major. "It's like the country along the chalk cliffs of southern England."

The major nodded. "Thank you, Miss."

Mr Buckmaster scanned the people at the table. "Any further questions?"

Heads shook and the meeting broke up.

Back in the car, Mr Buckmaster turned to me, frowning. "Miss Roberts, you were sent there as a radio operator not an investigator. You correctly decided not to go into the village but you failed in your decision to visit the barracks. If you'd been captured, it would have alerted the Germans to our interest in the area."

I sat in silence, not sure what to say as Mr Buckmaster's eyes bored into mine. I had felt cornered in France, but Mr Buckmaster wouldn't be interested in hearing that.

His face changed. "You felt you had to, hmm?"

I pursed my lips and then nodded, surprised by his understanding.

"It's a problem ..." He leaned back in the seat, huffing out a breath. "The *Maquis* depend on trust. If they don't trust us, we get nowhere." His eyes softened. "But you understand the risk you took – and its implications?"

"Yes, sir."

"Very well." His gaze rested on me for a second. "I think you made the correct decision."

I felt a knot of tension release. I needed his approval to be sent on another mission.

"Back at the office, you'll go through a standard debriefing. I expect you'll find it trying."

He was right.

The debriefing team of two experienced agents made me go through every minute of every day – multiple times. I described everything I saw and heard and they probed the inevitable inconsistencies in the retellings, exploring the reasons for any opinions I expressed. At the end of two and a half days of this, I felt flat and dry, like a sheet squeezed through a mangle to remove the water after a wash. I then went on leave, to report back to HQ on 12th January.

The days I spent back at Lyndhurst were surreal: the tension I had felt from everyone in France did not exist. In Lyndhurst, they acknowledged the war in rationing, reading the papers, listening to the BBC and the uniforms we saw everywhere, but the smouldering thread of fear that ran through everyone in France was absent. I had difficult conversations with my mother and grandparents when they tried to find out about my work that required civilian clothes. I hated telling them nothing, unable to share this part of my life with the people I loved, the people who loved me.

My father's understanding of my situation during his brief Christmas visit helped soothe their ruffled feathers. But walking Granny Roberts' dogs on my first day in Lyndhurst gave me perhaps the strangest experience of my leave: I assessed the sound of every approaching vehicle, constantly checking for escape routes and hiding places. I had been in France for a handful of days, yet those days had soaked far into the depths of my psyche. But by the end of my leave, that hyper-vigilance faded.

What if they were to send me back to France?

I dithered about what to wear when I reported back to HQ – uniform or civvies? My ID card and the pass to get me into Baker Street made no mention of my rank or service and so I decided to wear civvies and packed my uniform.

After reporting, I found myself back on the street heading for Wanborough Manor as an instructor where Major de Wesselow was still the CO. Once there, I discovered that I had to assess attendees – deciding if the people on the course should continue or RTU. I found judging people difficult. I knew my own struggle with self-doubt and I saw that in many of the men and women training at Wanborough; because of this, I dithered over my opinions at the first such meeting.

Major de Wesselow spoke sharply. "Miss Roberts, we are not asking you for certainty here, but for your opinions and the reasons behind them. Just tell us what you think and why."

After that I limited my comments by thinking things through before the meetings and trying to avoid being the first to speak. However, Major de Wesselow stuck to military protocol and always required the junior person – me – to speak first.

Being at Wanborough Manor allowed me to improve my firearms and explosives skills. I disliked shooting and would never excel – but I hit the target with increasing frequency no matter the weapon handed to me. My intuitive grasp of explosives remained and I moved on to the dangerous but fascinating task of creating booby traps, to the instructor's delight.

By the end of February, I began to think that whatever operation planned to capture the radar set at Bruneval had aborted for some reason as there'd been no news of such a raid. Then came the announcement of the great success of Operation Biting. Paratroopers had landed, killed or captured the guards and dismantled the RDF set, bringing it back to England by sea. Of course, the role of the *Maquis* had to remain secret to keep them safe from reprisal. I managed to be appropriately excited at the news – without letting on that I knew anything about it.

May 1942 – November 1944

In late May, I received orders to return to my previous role as a radio operator, but this time at the SOE's new radio centre in Grendon Underwood. I dug out my WAAF uniform and reported for duty. I kept my physical fitness by running and, as I searched my emotions, I found my trip to occupied France had evaporated my guilt and shame – but the scars from my earlier failure remained; beneath them lingered the remnants of those dark, destructive creatures that had so nearly consumed me. More secure in myself, I forged some friendships with a few of the girls I worked with. They tried to set me up with a few men, but I decided I had no time for romantic entanglements until after the war: I wanted to get back to France.

I remained at Grendon Underwood until November 1943, when they recalled me to Baker Street.

By this time, everyone knew that the invasion was coming – and I'm sure the *Boche* knew this too, but they had to guess where and when the blow would fall. They had to defend a coast from the Spanish border to Norway on their west flank and along the northern Mediterranean to the south – where they'd already lost ground in Italy.

The work of Section F ratcheted up. SAS (Special Air Service) patrols needed briefing about France and the *Maquis*. They had created mayhem and chaos behind enemy lines in north Africa and once the invasion started, they'd do the same in France. I went to various places in southern England – never on a military base – staying with each patrol for several days to brief them as they worked up for this task. They would operate independently from the *Maquis*, but they still needed to understand something about France and the Resistance: I provided that.

But there had been no mention of my direct involvement on the ground. The idea of returning to France to participate in its liberation stirred visceral fear of capture and what would follow... and yet I felt this irresistible need to go. Liberation also seduced me with elated visions of playing a part in it. Upon self-examination, I discovered I feared breaking under interrogation and betraying the cause. I did not fear the death that would follow.

Did my death truly matter so little to me?

After weeks of dithering, in January I summoned the courage to beard Mr Buckmaster in his Baker Street office.

"Sir – a word, please?"

Mr Buckmaster's eyes narrowed – I think he knew what I wanted to talk about. "Come in, Miss Roberts." He waved me to a chair in his office. "How can I help you?"

I struggled, trying to find a way to start. "Umm ... sir, I ... er ..."

Mr Buckmaster smiled. "You want to go back to France?

I nodded.

He leaned back in his chair. "Well, we need you to finish your work with the SAS."

"Yes, sir. But after that?"

He breathed out through steepled fingers. "You've done – and continue to do – your bit."

I remained silent. I wasn't sure about that. The operation to Bruneval had been a walk in the park compared to some of the whispered stories I'd heard.

We stared at one another before he leant forward with a sigh. "Okay, Colette. I'll think about it."

My stomach tightened. "Thank you, sir."

"No guarantees, mind." His face held a friendly glower. "Now, off you go and finish getting the SAS sorted."

"Yes, sir. Thank you, sir."

Working with the SAS had its moments. They held themselves in high esteem and some thought I must be there for their carnal benefit. Most backed off when turned down, but a few pushed harder. As I always took part in the physical jerks and unarmed combat training with them, the persistent men realised, despite my small size, I could defend myself if they tried it on – and my aptitude with explosives impressed them. Word percolated through the groups and I heard myself referred to as the Ice Maiden – and the amorous advances petered out.

As winter became spring, talk of the upcoming invasion dominated and my work with the SAS groups continued. Then in April with the SAS groups trained, I went to Manchester for my delayed parachute qualification, which meant a possible operational role for me. The faint beat of butterfly wings started in my stomach.

We commenced our training by jumping off walls onto palliasses and then graduated to jumping off the back of a slow-moving truck onto grass. We got hung in a parachute harness inside a hangar and learned how to control the parachute by pulling on the shrouds. For our qualifying jump we boarded a Stirling. If you refused to jump, according to rumours, they'd send you off to some terrible job in the middle of nowhere. Eight of us sat there as the aircraft accelerated down the runway and climbed to our drop location, each of us communing silently with our nerves as the noise made conversation impossible.

The red 'ready' light came on and we lined up, hooking on our static lines. The jump master checked us over. When he slid back the door, the rushing air roared as loud as the engines.

Green light.

I was number four. When number three jumped I took the position, hands on either side or the door. The airflow buffeted me and I gripped harder.

Smack.

The jump master's 'go' signal practically pushed me out of the plane – but I managed to push off with my feet, salvaging some of my pride. Sky and land whirled for a long moment of confused falling before the opening parachute jerked me upright. Below and behind I saw the chutes of the preceding jumpers and I grabbed the shrouds to try to steer myself into wind. The heath below accelerated towards me and I adopted the landing position, hit and rolled. The chute dragged me across the ground propelled by the wind, but I heaved on the shrouds to collapse it, helped by a gorse bush that snagged one side.

With its voluminous folds gathered somewhat securely in my arms, I headed for the waiting truck, waddling like a duck due to the parachute harness.

"Well done, Miss. Put your chute in the trailer."

I smiled at our instructor and doffed the harness, piling it and the chute into the cavernous trailer. Back at the base, they presented us with our parachute wings and hustled us off to the station to get trains to our postings. My orders had me headed back to Baker Street and Section F where I received orders to return to France, liaising with the *Maquis* in the Vosges, northeast France.

After some weeks of briefing and coding practice – poems were out and coding sheets printed on silk were in – I jumped from a Wellington on the night of 25th May 1944 near Saarebourg, west of Strasbourg, along with cannisters of equipment: arms and explosives for the *Maquis*. This time, I was Marie Gilles – a seventeen-year-old orphan from Strasbourg.

The parachute drop and link up with the Maquis went like clockwork. I retrieved my radio and bags from one of the cannisters dropped with me before the *Maquis* whisked them away. Two Frenchmen – Alain and Georges – led me off into the wooded hills. They had fled Saarebourg to avoid the forced labour draft. They based themselves in various dilapidated woodsman's huts scattered though the forested hills south of the town. We only stayed two nights in any one place, using dead letter drops to communicate to and fro with our information sources. Some people in this region close to the German border regarded themselves as German not French – which made things complicated and dangerous.

On 6th June, the allies landed in Normandy and the Vosges started to hope for liberation as the Allies first gained a beachhead and then ground their way inland through the Normandy *bocages*.

Alain and Georges picked up information from the dead drops and occasionally met with their contacts, returning with reports that I coded and transmitted. There were rumours that the *Boche* might reinforce the Vosges – but we had no solid information. In one message, I sent back the location of a concentration camp at nearby Natzweiler into which *Maquis* prisoners disappeared, never to be seen again.

Radioing back information presented problems, in part because the hills restricted the radio signal but also because the wooded, hilly terrain with few tracks and no roads offered few easy escape routes. Many routes were little better than animal tracks, but Alain and Georges knew the wooded hills well and found safe transmission locations for me; I sent my short messages, recorded any response and we scooted off. We knew the *SD* had listening vans based in Saarebourg, but they had to stay on the few roads. One of the return messages told us the *SD* were aware of a new transmitter in the Vosges. All we could do was shrug at the news and carry on, moving locations after each transmission.

By mid-August, the allies had broken out, stormed across France and liberated Paris. The Nazis were streaming back towards Germany in a retreat that was almost a rout. Our excitement rose and we talked about welcoming allied troops. We fed back what information we had about troop movements as the Nazis retreated.

The radio came with a hand-powered dynamo to recharge the battery, but on 20th August it stopped working after Alain dropped it. We cranked the dynamo, heard it whirring – but no current came. I now had a radio with enough charge for one transmit and listen session.

I hefted the wretched object in my hands. "We need to charge the batteries and get this fixed."

Georges shook his head. "That means a visit to a town with a repair shop we trust."

"Is there such a place near here?"

Alain and Georges exchanged a look.

"I think so, in Saarebourg." Alain rubbed his chin. "If we move near to Arzviller, we can slip you into town from there."

Georges looked long and hard at Alain. They couldn't enter the town as the *Boche* watched out for able-bodied men for the forced labour program.

Georges frowned. "Frederic's garage? Is he still there?"

Alain shrugged. "It's been some months, but I've not heard it's closed."

Georges' face clouded with doubt.

Alain stared back at him. "But we'd have heard if something had happened."

Georges sniffed and turned to me. "Why not radio for another dynamo?"

I pondered our options. "Perhaps – but that uses up the battery and it might take a week to send a new dynamo. That would leave us with no way of transmitting again until it arrived." I thought hard. "It's better to get it fixed and charge the battery in town at the same time. That way there'll be enough charge to ask for a replacement dynamo if they can't fix it." They'd sent a Eureka homing beacon as part of my equipment, which made accurate drops easier.

Despite much discussion, no better plan emerged. Overnight, we moved close to Arzviller, a small village not far from Saarebourg.

Outside Arzviller, I met Sylvie, a woman in her twenties. She would take me to the garage and introduce me to Frederic. I left the radio and silk coding cloth as too dangerous to carry into town, removing the battery to take with us. We then spent some hours in the forest gathering sacks of pinecones. We hid the battery and dynamo in two of these, wrapped in old clothes and placed amongst the pinecones. The townsfolk purchased and used pinecones as kindling.

Sylvie and I set off towards the town along the quiet, dusty road pushing a handcart carrying the sacks of pinecones with the two important ones at the bottom. It was a warm day and we were soon sweating from our exertions. About halfway to town, a Wehrmacht car drew ahead of us, and stopped. An officer climbed out and sauntered back to us, leaving the driver standing beside the car.

"Hello, pretty girls." He leered at us, speaking French with a thick German accent.

Sylvie and I exchanged a glance. I was conscious of our pistols, hidden on a shelf at the back of the cart.

"Come, come, pretty girls." He smiled as his eyes roved greasily over us. "Nothing to say to a handsome officer?"

Sylvie wiped the sweat off her brow with a cloth from the back of the cart. "We need to get to Saarebourg, sir. Our families depend on us selling these pinecones there."

"Are you refusing my company?" His eyes narrowed.

Sylvie shook her head. "No, sir." She glanced at me. "Why not share a glass of wine with us in town when we get there?"

The officer stood surveying us for a moment, his face darkening. He grabbed a sack of pinecones, upending it onto the road. "No here. Now."

He dragged another sack off the cart. The next one held the dynamo.

I glanced at Sylvie, who leant down, putting the cloth on the shelf where our pistols rested.

"Please sir. Please don't make us pick up all the pinecones again." I pleaded.

The officer turned towards me with a cruel smile and reached for the sack, staggering sideways when Sylvie's pistol spoke.

I grabbed my pistol and saw the driver lean into the car. I ran forward and fired twice as I'd been trained. To my amazement, the driver dropped into the dust beside the car. I heard another shot behind me – Sylvie finishing off the officer, I supposed.

I bent down, checking the driver: dead. One of my shots had gone into his skull through an eye. I gulped queasily at the bloody mess and started to stand up.

Something cold press against my neck. "Drop the gun."

For a moment, I froze. The pistol pushed hard into my neck.

"Drop it. Now."

I dropped the pistol and a boot kicked me forward, sprawling me onto the road away from my pistol. Above me, I saw the officer, a patch of blood growing on his left sleeve.

He gestured me away from the car with his pistol. "Move there and kneel."

I shuffled across and knelt where he pointed. He backed towards the car, pistol waving in my direction and leaned down, checking the driver, kicking my pistol and the driver's under the car.

"Now we'll see what's hidden amongst those pinecones." His pistol waved me towards the handcart. "Tip them on the ground."

I moved towards the cart, where Sylvie sprawled unmoving in a large pool of blood, her throat torn open by the officer's shot. I could see her pistol, a meter or so from the cart.

A jolt of anger at Sylvie spiked through me.

How had she let this happen? She had her pistol in hand when the officer did not.

The officer saw me look at the pistol. "Kick the gun towards me."

If I kicked it hard enough, perhaps it'd go off...

"Be careful." He winced in pain but his pistol remained pointing at me.

I shuffled the pistol about a couple of meters closer to him.

"Excellent." His pistol waved me back to the cart. "Now tip out the bags."

I hesitated.

The pistol tightened its aim. "Now."

I picked up the first of the two remaining bags and tipped it onto the road. The bundle holding the dynamo shouted its difference as it thudded on the road.

The officer glanced at the bundle and then back at me, a sardonic eyebrow raised. "And ..."

A moment later, the battery bundle lay close to the dynamo.

The sound of an approaching vehicle interrupted us. A *Wehrmacht* truck rolled round the corner and stopped with a squeal of brakes, the driver unsure of the scene before him.

"Get down here and arrest this girl." The officer's face was white and blood was now dripping from his left arm.

Rough hands grabbed me and I felt rope bind my hands behind my back. The officer leant against the front of the truck and one of the soldiers helped him off with his jacket and bandaged his upper arm, securing it in a sling.

"Open those bundles." He pointed at the battery and dynamo in their cloth wrapping, lying on the road

One of the soldiers approached them warily.

"Get on with it." The officer jerked his head in my direction. "She dropped them on the road so they won't explode."

The soldier unwrapped the bundles revealing the contents.

The officer looked at them and then turned to me, a knowing smile playing on his lips. He gestured at the battery and dynamo. "Put them in my car. I will need one of your men to drive me with this person into Saarebourg."

The *Feldwebel* organised soldiers to toss the bodies of Sylvie and the driver into the back of the truck.

The officer pointed at me. "Search her then put her in the back of the car." As he turned away, I saw the *SD* sleeve flash – the intelligence branch of the *SS*. Hands groped my body and I saw the lust in the searcher's eyes. All he found was my ID Card which he handed to the officer.

Ten minutes later, the car stopped in the yard behind the SD building. They dragged me out, frogmarched me through to the cells and shoved me into one. I stumbled across the cell, just managing to turn so it was my shoulder not my face that crashed into the wall. I slumped onto the floor as the steel door slammed shut.

I shivered at my future.

I'd been through practice interrogations ... enough to see me through? Could I stay silent until I drifted away as I had done before?

I tried to breathe calmness into myself, but fear kept spiking through. Sometime later, a guard arrived to remove the rope binding my hands as another watched from the doorway. Again, I was shoved at the wall as the guard left. No word was spoken. Somehow, I slept, punctuated by dark dreams. I lay awake for a while before they came for me.

They dragged me into a room and strapped me tightly to a chair and left.

Time passed and I sat in silence before the SD officer walked in, his arm in a sling. Accompanying him was a large soldier carrying a bucket, water slopping over the brim.

I knew what that was for ...

The officer smiled despite the sling on his left arm. "Now, Marie, I hope we can continue without further unpleasantness."

I sat in silence, my eyes locked on his.

His smirk changed to a cruel and arrogant smile. "A battery and broken dynamo for a radio ... and you are the radio operator, not the dead girl." He paused, savouring his victory. "Her family is currently enjoying the hospitality of the *Gestapo*."

I was glad Sylvie was beyond their grasp – but her family had ended up in the Nazi's terrible maw ...

"We've heard your transmissions up in the hills for a while now and have been trying to find you." He smiled. "So kind of you to drop in and save us further trouble." The officer's voice hardened. "Now you will tell us who has been helping you, where they live and where you've hidden your radio."

There was no-one and nothing to hide behind. Fear of what was to come filled my mouth with saliva. I nearly swallowed, signalling my fear. I spat at him instead.

He examined the spittle that had landed on his boot.

"I see." He signalled the soldier. "Do not damage her ... too much."

The soldier removed his jacket and, with a leer, grabbed the neck of my dress, ripping it off my shoulders and open to the waist. The officer's lascivious eyes slid over my breasts. The soldier picked up a metre length of rubber pipe and lashed each breast in turn.

After the agonising blows, the officer repeated the questions – and I spat, again.

***

I remember it all: the incessant questions some yelled, others whispered into my ear, the beatings, the suffocations, the rapes.

But the details don't matter.

What matters is ... I held my silence. During each session I drifted from my body, to watch and not speak. The interrogation was days long – two, three ... four? I lost count.

In the grey dawn of a morning, the cell door crashed open. A guard threw down beside my naked body striped pants and a jacket with a large red X on the back. "Dress."

The material was coarse and grated across my damaged skin. I struggled into the pants with difficulty as I was stiff and aching. The guards grabbed me and one forced my arms into the jacket, ignoring my groans as he stretched damaged muscles and torn skin.

At the railyard they shoved me into a cattle wagon full of women, slamming the door behind me. The women saw my battered condition and tried to ease my pain. We were in that wagon for two days with neither food nor water, sometimes clattering along but also stationary for hours on end. When they slid back the door one afternoon and yelled at us to get out, we found the guards were women.

Pushed and prodded, threatened by slavering dogs, we shuffled towards the gates of a compound. Inside, we stood in ranks, shivering in the icy wind blowing off a nearby lake.

One of the guards spotted the red X on my jacket, calling out and pointing at me.

They hauled me out of line – a special prisoner, it seemed – dragged me across to the main camp building where I ended up in another bleak cell.

In the morning, a girl in the striped prison uniform worked her way down the cells, emptying our stinking slop buckets accompanied by an SS guard. Later she brought a meagre amount of food and water to each of us. We shared brief, furtive looks through the meal hatch before I tried speaking – but she understood neither English nor French.

I pointed to myself. "Englander."

What was the German for French?

She blinked and checked down the corridor, wary of the guards, and then pointed to herself. "*Deutsch* ... Frida."

She was German. What had a German child done to warrant imprisonment in such a place?

I pointed to myself. "Colette." After a moment I flashed twenty-two fingers, pointed to myself and then her. She showed me fifteen fingers. I had thought her younger, but then she was half-starved, showing every bone beneath her pale skin.

She glanced sideways again and scrambled away as I heard boots approaching.

Over the following days Frida's stops at my meal hatch lengthened and we held frustratingly broken conversations, learning words in those stolen minutes. The day after I arrived, she told me of two other SOE girls in the cells by pointing to me and then down the corridor twice. A week or so later I was the sole remaining SOE girl. Accompanied by a strutting SS officer, guards dragged the two past my cell and through a door at the corridor's end. I heard two gunshots.

At least they hadn't died alone ...

But time with Frida was minutes in long hours of isolation. Dr Johnson had quipped that the knowledge of impending execution concentrated the mind. I set out in what time I had left to relive my happy memories, slipping away from my dank and freezing cell to ... picnics in the Bois de Boulogne and the gardens at Versailles, to strolling with my parents beside the Seine in the shimmering wet streets of Paris. I relived glorious summer days with my cousins on the beaches of Normandy – memories now clouded by the knowledge of the furious battles fought there just months ago.

And those memories led me to the success of my first operation at Bruneval and on to the reports I sent back from the Vosges.

I had played my part. I had helped liberate France.

July – August 1975

"Camille?"

I looked up from the novel I was reading. "Yes, my love?"

My husband, David, was holding a letter that trembled in his hands. "Perhaps ... a clue about Colette."

We never knew what had happened to our daughter after she was captured. She had been interrogated at the SD offices in Saarebourg but after that the trail went cold. In the aftermath of the war, I searched the records I could find, even visiting the nearby Natzweiler-Struthof Concentration camp in the Vosges but there was no record of Colette there, nor did the people I found who survived that place recall her being there. I did manage to find and speak with one of the men she had worked with – Alain.

Through him we learned more of the circumstances surrounding her capture. Colette was going into town with another girl to have repairs made to the radio's dynamo, but they never made it. Their capture was bad luck – a case of being in the wrong place at the wrong time. After a brief gun battle in which the girl died, Colette was captured and taken to Saarebourg, where she was interrogated.

I tried not to think about what happened to her there.

After Saarebourg, we had been unable to find any trace of her.

"Camille?"

I blinked back into the present. "Sorry. Yes?"

"A historian has been going through some jumbled Nazi papers in Strasbourg and came across a reference to Colette."

I stood up. "We need to go and meet him, look at the papers."

David smiled. "Her." He looked back down at the letter. "Jean-Marie Buisson. There's a phone number. I'll see if we can go and meet her."

***

We took the train from Paris and spent a day in Strasbourg, meeting with Jean-Marie. She had found only one document relating to Colette – a page from the Saarebourg SD records – listing Colette as a prisoner. The page had suffered water damage, so some of the entry was almost illegible. There appeared to be something stamped beside her entry – but we couldn't make it out. With Jean-Marie's permission, I took several photographs of the page and had them developed back in Paris. Even blown up, we could not make out the stamp.

A few weeks later, the phone rang. "Madame Roberts?"

"Yes."

"It's Mademoiselle Buisson. I have found a reference to a person being transferred from Saarebourg to Ravensbrück concentration camp about a week after your daughter was captured."

I waved across the room at David. "There's no name mentioned?"

"No, I'm afraid not ... but the date is about right for it to be your daughter."

I mouthed 'Colette' at David as he moved to my side. "And there's nothing else?"

"Not so far. But I will contact you if I find anything else." Mademoiselle Buisson's voice was full of sympathy.

"Thank you so much."

I put the phone down, realising that David was holding my other hand. "Someone was moved from Saarebourg to Ravensbrück concentration camp at about the time Colette disappeared."

David sighed. "Perhaps this is nothing ... just another dead end."

I shrugged. "Perhaps ... but perhaps not."

David stroked my arm. "We'll go to Ravensbrück, then?"

"Let me make some enquiries first."

But Colette's name did not appear on the Ravensbrück prisoner lists, such as were available without a personal visit. We discovered there was a rededication of the camp memorial in August and a new museum opening – if we went there, we could inspect the records in person.

I had stared at the photograph from the SD records for hours before I thought perhaps the illegible stamp was NA or maybe NN – but I had no idea what either could mean.

We travelled by train to Berlin and then north to Ravensbrück, staying in the town. We had arranged access to the records held at the camp, but after a day's work there was still no trace of Colette. We went to the rededication the following morning which was attended by about a hundred former inmates.

David and I then walked round the camp, ending up in the *Kommandantur*. As we walked down the cell corridor, a family group with a young child in a pusher was in front of us. The older woman dropped to her knees in front of one of the cell doors, scrabbling at the meal hatch.

One of the museum staff spoke to her in German and she stopped. The young man in the group offered the woman a hand up, speaking in German – but I understood one word – "Colette" and nearly staggered.

David's hand tightened on my arm.

He leant towards the woman. "Excuse me ... did you just mention ... Colette?"

The woman turned, scanning across the people nearby and speaking English. "Who just asked about Colette?"

David glanced at me. "Umm ... that was me. Did you know Colette – an English SOE girl?"

"Please forgive me, but who are you to be asking about Colette?" The woman's voice hinted at suspicion.

I drew myself up. "We are Colette Roberts' parents." I returned her suspicious look. "Who are you?"

She must have heard my French accent as she switched to French. "I am Frida Schmidt." She slid a finger across a name badge I had not noticed. "I was imprisoned here as a child. The Nazis had me working in these cells for the final year of the war." She bared her left arm, showing her blue prisoner number. "Colette started teaching me English."

We gazed into each other's eyes, finding the hurt buried there.

I swallowed. "There's more, isn't there?"

Our eyes stayed locked then she turned back to the museum guide, speaking in German. After a brief exchange, the guide walked back down the corridor.

Mrs Schmidt turned to the young woman with her and guided her forward. "Please allow me to introduce my daughter, Colette, named to honour your courageous daughter."

I nodded at the woman but grasped Mrs Schmidt's arm. "Do you know what happened to our Colette?"

Mrs Schmidt's face was full of sorrow. "I don't know what had happened to her before she came here." She stopped for a moment, searching her memory. "It was sometime in September 1944 that she arrived here."

David told her about Colette's mission in the Vosges, what we knew about her capture, the SD prisoner list stamped with NA or NN and the faint lead to Ravensbrück that brought us here.

Mrs Schmidt's daughter gave the young man a meaningful look and he turned, pushing his daughter up the corridor. Just then the guide returned and there was another brief conversation in German before Mrs Schmidt turned back to me. "The stamp would be 'NN' – it means *Nacht und Nebel* – night and fog. This was stamped on the files of people who were to disappear without trace. It was part of the Nazi's terror tactics."

Mrs Schmidt enfolded my hand in hers. "You know Colette is dead and there will be no grave?"

In my head I knew Colette was dead – but this gentle telling pushed the knowing into my heart, choked my throat and set tears in my eyes. I summoned strength from somewhere and gave her a brief nod.

"My daily morning task was slopping out the cells." Mrs Schmidt explained. "When I arrived that morning, Colette's cell door was open – with no guard outside."

Her gentle grasp on my hands firmed for a moment.

"I knew what that meant."

Our eyes locked. I could see the cost to her in this retelling, but I needed more.

Mrs Schmidt read my face. "A few minutes after I arrived, an SS officer came back through that door." She gestured towards the end of the corridor. "He saw me standing in tears at Colette's cell and mocked me for mourning a spy, pinning me by the throat against the wall with a hand that stank from the gunshot."

Emotion surged between us through our eyes and hands.

"The SS officer was Vogel." Mrs Schmidt's eyes slid shut for a moment and a tremor ran through her. "Somehow, he escaped the attentions of the Allies at the end of the war. He turned up in Australia where I recognised his photo in a newspaper." There was a flicker of something else on her face, but it was gone in a moment. "He disappeared after that and is presumed to have died when they found his car abandoned."

David slid his arm round my shoulder.

Mrs Schmidt tapped the steel door. "This was Colette's cell – and if you wish, we can go to the execution yard where ..." She stopped, taking a breath, mastering the emotions threatening to overwhelm her. "That man ended your brave and beautiful daughter's life."

David looked down at me and I nodded as a shiver passed through me.

The guide opened the door, revealing a small yard with concrete walls and an earth floor. Opposite was another door.

As our small group walked into the yard, emotion conquered Mrs Schmidt. She collapsed to her knees, a silent wail ending in wracking sobs. Reliving these memories was torturing this poor woman – and I was doing it to her. I fell to my knees beside her, shameful tears running down my face, my arm round her shoulder. A moment later another arm joined mine; her daughter knelt with us.

We merged into a tight group, sharing our breath and tears. I found a tissue in my bag and wiped Mrs Schmidt's face. This close, I could see she was decades younger than me – she must have been just a girl when imprisoned here. "My dear, what you've been through."

After a while, her eyes opened full of strange calmness.

"Thank you for being our daughter's friend." I swallowed down the emotions now threatening to overwhelm me. "Thank you for sharing with us your part in her story."

David reached down, giving me a much-needed hand, lifting me to my feet as her daughter helped her mother to hers.

Mrs Schmidt reached for my hand again. "It was your daughter and a couple of other SOE girls who started teaching me English." Her eyes shone with tears. "They all knew their fate and yet they never showed me their fear." She continued after several breaths. "A bond developed with your daughter. I used to sit outside her cell, talking through the meal hatch ..."

We shared a thin, sad smile. "And you named your daughter in her memory." I clasped her hand in gratitude. "Thank you."

"She deserves so much more ..."

My gaze wandered down the grim corridor. "I'm sure that's true for the thousands herded into this place."

David held me against his shoulder as Mrs Schmidt and her daughter murmured quietly. There was something different about her now – a release, perhaps, of the horrors she had carried from here.

I nudged David. "Please, give her our card so we can stay in touch."

Mrs Schmidt smiled as she took the card and I leant in, kissing her on both cheeks. "*Merci*."

We shared a look and then I turned and, holding David close, we walked back down the corridor where our daughter spent her last days.

Tears of prideful sorrow blurred my sight and I leant my head against David's shoulder. "Colette played her part in bringing this horror to an end."

David's hand reached up, smoothing the tears from my cheek. Outside, the bright sunlight glinted from the moisture in his eyes and we clasped one another sharing our love and loss.

Afterword

This story is fiction – but wound round real characters and historical events.

Maurice Buckmaster was the head of Section F at the Special Operations Executive HQ at 64 Baker Street in London. I wonder if it amused the SOE to share a street with the most famous British fictional detective. Somewhat inevitably, the SOE were referred to as "Baker Street Irregulars" in some quarters.

Operation Biting was a real operation that captured a new short-range German radar system from Bruneval in late February 1942. That operation was led by Major John Frost who later distinguished himself by leading the unit that, in September 1944, took and held the Arnhem Bridge for days against units of the 9th SS Panzer division during the ill-fated Operation Market Garden. Colonel Rémy (real name Gilbert Renault) was a significant member of the French Resistance and provided some information needed for Operation Biting. SAS troops were used behind enemy lines after D-day to disrupt the enemy, including in the Vosges.

But Colette Roberts is complete fiction. She initially occurs as a brief mention in my first novel *Through my Eyes. Again.* and then again in the sequel *Through different Eyes*. It was the latter mention that led to this story.

I needed a description of events around Colette's execution at Ravensbrück concentration camp for Mutti Frida to relate to her daughter, who is named Colette in honour of the SOE agent. In order to do that, I wrote the first draft of the scene that opens this story and then wrote Mutti Frida's retelling of her interaction with Vogel in *Through different Eyes*.

After writing Colette's execution, a very strange thing happened: this fictional, French/English woman stood by my side for days, quietly insisting I tell her story – and *Colette* is the result.

Opening with an execution might be considered melodramatic – and having the victim relating her own execution is unusual – but that's the way it came out. I tried putting the execution at the end – but it just did not feel right. Perhaps in part the opening was my subconscious desire to warn readers that this story would stray into some dark and difficult territory: Colette's capture and violent interrogation at the hands of the Nazis.

But when I reached that part of the story, I found I could not write it. For two weeks, I stared at the stationary blinking cursor, unable find a way to write the horrific reality of what she would have experienced. It would be too easy to become a voyeur of her suffering or trivialise the reality that too many experienced.

I reread a torture and interrogation scene of a young woman written brilliantly by a writing friend, but I knew I could not write a scene like that. Finally, I realised Colette did not have to relate what they did to her. I went back through the story, adding her experiences in practice interrogations. From my SOE research, these practice sessions were at least as intense as I have described. Finally, Colette watched her interrogation and torture at the hands of the Nazis from a distance, from outside her body.

I learned French and German at school and fell in love with Verlaine's poetry. I chose *Chanson d'automne* as Colette's coding poem because I love its melancholy evocation of autumn, foreboding endings. It feels right for Colette, who struggled against feelings of helplessness – but found a way through, unlike Verlaine. Since choosing the poem, I have discovered that the opening lines were used as codes on the BBC to alert the *Maquis* – the French Resistance – to the coming D-Day invasion.

Forty-one Section F women served in occupied France during WW2, sixteen of them died in that service, almost all executed at one or other concentration camp, including Ravensbrück – the only all-female Nazi concentration camp.

I have visited Europe many times and on one such visit, after prevaricating for years, I finally summoned the courage to visit a concentration camp – Dachau, near Munich. Even in the bright sunshine of a summer's day, it is a bleak reminder of humanity's darkest abilities. In the crematorium a plaque commemorates four SOE girls, executed there on 12th September 1944. Amidst all the deaths that occurred there (an estimated 50,000) it was that plaque and those deaths that undammed my tears.

Memorial plaque in the Dachau concentration camp crematorium

In part, this story is my tribute to those courageous women who went willingly into the darkness of occupied Europe. Women who were prepared to purchase fascism's defeat with their own lives.

Robert Hart

Brisbane, Australia

2022

Chanson d'Automne

Paul Verlaine

Les sanglots longs
Des violons
De l'automne
Blessent mon cœur
D'une langueur
Monotone.
Tout suffocant
Et blême, quand
Sonne l'heure,
Je me souviens
Des jours anciens
Et je pleure;
Et je m'en vais
Au vent mauvais
Qui m'emporte
Deçà, delà,
Pareil à la
Feuille morte.

The song of Autumn

The long laments of autumn's violins
Wound my heart with a dreary listlessness.
Breathless and pale as the hour sounds,
I recall the old days and cry;
And I leave on the ill wind that carries me
Here and there like a dead leaf.

Translation by Robert Hart 2022.

Did you love *Colette*? Then you should read *Through my Eyes. Again.*[1] by Robert Hart!

It is 1962 and Will Johnstone is sent back to his twelve-year-old body. What's more, he is about to escape his abusive father … by committing suicide. Will recoils from the act, resuming his troubled but jarringly changed life. Helped by unexpected allies, he sets out to rescue himself. Through his friendship with Col, the son of an East German defector, Will is swept into events at the edge of a different Cold War – events that threaten to rip apart his life – and heart.

A timeslip novel set in Europe during an alternative Cold War.

1. https://books2read.com/u/mgzYg6

2. https://books2read.com/u/mgzYg6

Also by Robert Hart

Through my Eyes. Again.
Mrs Henderson's Limp
Colette

About the Author

Robert was educated in the UK but emigrated to Australia after completing a degree in aerospace. He currently lives in Brisbane but has also lived in Melbourne and the Pilbara region in Australia and in the USA. He has worked in research and information systems and is currently teaching Mathematics and Physics. He is married, with two children, one grandson and several step grandchildren. He shares his day-to-day life with his wife, Rozz, two ginger cats (Hypatia and Eratosthenes) and a black labradoodle (Ana).

He loves classical music (particularly opera) as does his wife and satisfies his life-long love affair with flying by soaring in gliders. His longest flight is over 800km and he is still trying to fly over 1000 km in a single flight.

Advance notice: *Through different Eyes,* the sequel to *Through my Eyes. Again.* is underway with publication expected in mid 2022.